BETTING ON THE BIRD
FIXER UPPER ROMANCE #1.5: A SAPPHIC CHRISTMAS ROM COM

CASSANDRA MEDCALF

Copyright © 2022 by Cassandra Medcalf

All rights reserved.

No part of this book may be reproduced in any form or by any electronic or mechanical means, including information storage and retrieval systems, without written permission from the author, except for the use of brief quotations in a book review.

This novel is a work of fiction. The names, characters, and incidents portrayed in it are the work of the author's imagination. Any resemblance to actual persons, living or dead, events, or localities is entirely coincidental.

Cover created by Ashley Santoro.

ISBN

E-Book: 979-8985531756

Paperback: 979-8-9855317-6-3

To all the readers and reviewers who left me feedback on my first-ever book as a self-published author: this is dedicated to you. I hope you enjoy Bonnie and Natalie's much-deserved Christmas romance.

CHAPTER 1

Natalie Roche thrust her hip into the pantry door, packing away the broom, Clorox wipes, and vacuum after cleaning up in anticipation for Bonnie's return from the grocery store. She'd finally managed to clear off the dining room table of all the junk mail, hardware store catalogs, and moving debris from the past three months, and even dug out the festive tablecloth and silver candlesticks from the attic in preparation.

This Christmas dinner was going to put Norman Rockwell to shame.

She ran once more through the December checklist on her phone while taking one last loop around the downstairs.

Singing Reindeer wreath hung on the front door? Check.

Chimney swept and wood stacked for a delightful holiday fire? Check.

Bonnie's present tucked safely away in the hall closet behind the wrapping paper and the baby stuff she'd picked out for Ethan and Clara?

Check, and check.

Natalie looked around at her grandmother's sparkling clean

house, almost ready for the holidays. Later this week, Shawn would be coming over to get the lights strung outside (something Natalie had *wanted* to finish weeks ago, but had been forced to wait while Shawn replaced the gutters). And once her seven-foot pre-lit tree came in the mail—*damn holiday back orders*—this place would sparkle with the festive spirit Natalie had come to crave like clockwork every holiday season.

When she'd first read her grandmother's letter after accepting her inheritance, she hadn't been so sure that she'd be able to fulfill her dying wish to make this house her home, especially after being away for so long. But she'd be darned if the spirit of Christmas wasn't really making it come to fruition.

It was different, here, in the Blue Ridge Mountains. There was a definite chill in the air now that it was December, and Bonnie had even taken Natalie to the Outlets last week to get her "an actual winter coat." After living in L.A. for most of her adulthood, Natalie had been woefully unprepared for a real winter. Jean jackets and designer cardigans didn't cut it for a winter in western Maryland, so Bonnie had taken it upon herself to revamp Natalie's wardrobe to get her ready for the holidays.

Meanwhile, Natalie took it upon herself to educate Bonnie in the traditions of a Southern California Christmas: decorating.

The outlets had given her a taste of some Christmas energy, but Natalie missed the ginormous trees and light displays of the Glendale Galleria. She longed for a spa weekend in Vegas to take selfies with the holiday-themed Venetian Glass displays and the Bellagio fountains. As a young adult finding her way in the world, the obnoxious consumerist displays of Christmas and expensive workplace holiday parties had been enough to help her forget that she wouldn't have a white Christmas or family to open presents with.

In fact, this was the first year since she was in college that she'd be seeing her family at all for the holidays. At last, she was going to fulfill the other part of her grandmother's dying wish: rebuilding her family. All Sophie Roche had wanted was for her grandkids to get along: a big, happy family that got together for the holidays and celebrated with big dinners and warm traditions. This was Natalie's first Christmas with her half-brother, Ethan: her big chance to reunite her long-lost family for the holidays. To win him over for good and honor her grandmother's memory.

She wasn't asking for too much. Truly. She was just insistent that everything be absolutely perfect and live up to every single one of her expectations for the big day.

"Nat, can you help me with this?"

Bonnie was balancing six reusable grocery bags in one hand, a giant cardboard package in the other and about to break off the heel of her shoe in an attempt to nudge the door open.

"On it!" Natalie called as she lunged for the front door. The *new* front door.

She jostled the box out of Bonnie's arm and twisted out of the way as she ushered her in through the door, lingering in the foyer as she checked the return address. "I think this is the tree!" She called out to Bonnie, who rushed the heavy bags to the kitchen.

"Cool, can you help me put away the frozen stuff?" Bonnie called back.

Natalie set the box down in the foyer and hurried to help unpack all the groceries. Though it made her girlfriend a little nervous, Natalie had insisted on hosting the Christmas dinner this year with her new-found family. It was going to be Bonnie, Natalie, her half-brother Ethan, and his pregnant wife Clara. She was going to cook a magnificent feast, starting with a beautiful organic heritage turkey she'd ordered special for the occasion, and ending with her signature peanut butter crème pie. She was going to gift Ethan the boxes of their dad's old baby things she'd found in the attic. And she was going to unofficially-officially come out to them and introduce Bonnie as her girlfriend. Which she'd only avoided doing because she'd been waiting for the dust to settle on the inheritance battle that Bonnie (as their grandmother's estate attorney) had overseen.

It was going to be perfect. Flawless! It was a flawless, perfect plan. Even if she had had to move things around to make sure everyone could attend. They'd decided it wasn't *actually* going to be on Christmas Day, but on December 23rd instead. Which was even better, actually. Christmas was on a Monday this year, after all, and who wants to plan a momentous holiday dinner for a Monday?

This Saturday, she was going to use those casserole recipes she found on Pinterest to serve along with the turkey and pie to make the greatest Christmas dinner anyone had ever had, and they were going to be a perfect happy family and live perfectly happily ever after. Just like Sophie Roche has always wanted.

Because it was Christmas. And that's how Christmas worked.

Bonnie tapped the toe of her shoe on the brittle linoleum floor as she looked at all the bags.

"Oh shit. We don't have a turkey," she said, slapping a hand to her forehead.

"We do! It's coming in the mail. I got us one of those fancy, eighteen-pound heritage turkeys from Maine."

"Eighteen pounds? It's only going to be the four of us."

At that moment, Natalie's cell phone rang in her pocket. *Mom.*

"Hello?"

"Natalie, darling," Michelle's voice rang through the phone. The white noise that accompanied it let Natalie know that her mother was calling while driving. "I just realized that this Sunday is Christmas Eve."

She pulled the phone away and put her on speaker so the car noise didn't blast directly in her ear. "Yeah?"

"So that isn't going to work for our usual Sunday dinner, is it?"

Since Natalie had returned from L.A., she and her mother had been working to patch their frayed relationship by having weekly dinners every Sunday. It was one of the only days Michelle didn't insist on working.

"Um... well, it wouldn't be the worst thing in the world to spend Christmas Eve together." She shot Bonnie an annoyed look. She shrugged.

"But all the restaurants are closed."

Of course. Michelle and her beloved restaurants. Natalie wasn't sure she even owned a refrigerator in her posh Bethesda condo.

"Well, you know..." Natalie took a breath and looked hopefully at Bonnie. Recognition dawned on her face, and immediately her girlfriend started crossing and uncrossing her arms across her chest, vehemently miming the universal sign for *ah, hell no!* "Um, I was going to make a Christmas Dinner on Saturday for Ethan and his wife, and a few of my... friends. You're welcome to come to that."

A moment of silence stretched across the line. Bonnie gaped at her, horrified.

"Ethan has a wife?" The background noise had lessened slightly, and it only highlighted the iciness of her tone.

"Yes, Clara. They're expecting. So I thought, it would be nice for them if they didn't have to cook a giant..." Natalie drifted off. Her mother likely didn't actually care at all about Ethan's family, considering he wasn't actually related to her at all. Ethan was part of the collection of secrets that Natalie's father had kept from Michelle, decades ago, that had destroyed *their* family.

"Well. That's very... *gracious* of you." She couldn't tell if Michelle's tone was complimentary or sarcastic.

"Thanks. Well. 'Tis the Season, and all."

"Right." Another pause. "I'd love to come."

"Really?" Nat squeaked. Bonnie groaned.

"Yes. I'll see you then. Kisses."

"Bye, mo–" the phone screen flashed "Call Ended" before she could finish. She turned to Bonnie. "I...guess there will be five of us on Saturday."

"No. Nat. *No*. Please tell me you *didn't* just invite your vindictive mother to Christmas dinner with Ethan and his very, very pregnant wife!" Bonnie wailed, holding two packs of thick-cut bacon threateningly. "That's a *terrible* idea!"

"*Vindictive* is a little strong," Natalie defended. Although she could understand why Bonnie felt that way. It was Michelle's fault that Natalie had lost touch with her father's side of the family and never even knew she'd had a half-brother in the first place. If she'd shared that little detail with her earlier in her life, she may have actually made an effort to come home and visit during her twenties. Maybe. "I mean, she's getting better. You got everything on the list didn't you?"

"Yes, I did, because you asked me to. But..." Bonnie's brow furrowed. She paused, crossing to the fridge to pile cream cheese into the deli drawer, and then turned back to face her girlfriend. She pinched her nose and took a deep breath, and looked like she was holding back much more than she actually ended up saying.

"I worry you're placing a little too much importance on this Christmas dinner."

Natalie knelt down and dug into the bags to unearth the rest of the frozen items and put them away. "Why would you say that?"

"Christmas is just a day, Nat. It doesn't have to be more or less important than any other day. And your family... well, there's a lot to unpack with your family. More than one dinner can accomplish."

Natalie closed the freezer and sat back on her heels. "Bonnie. I've told you how important this is to me."

The beautiful lawyer tapped over and took a knee beside her girlfriend, "I'm just saying, this doesn't have to be some big, perfect family reunion. You don't owe your mother a Christmas dinner. You don't have to come out to your brother if you don't want to yet. And you certainly don't have to tell him that you're romantically involved with the attorney that helped convince you to keep his grandmother's house!"

Her voice had risen. Bonnie paused and rubbed her hands over her face and her expression softened slightly. "I'm really nervous about how your family is going to take this. Can't I just be your *friend* until next year?" When she said the word "friend," she used air quotes. Natalie cringed. "Until you're more comfortable with your mom. Until you actually have a relationship with your brother. We've only been dating a couple of months, and I worry that you're putting a lot of pressure on yourself—on *us*—when you don't have to."

Natalie snorted. "I mean, Bonnie, we basically live together. We're *not* just friends—we're serious. Serious enough that I should tell my family."

"If they already knew you were gay, I'd agree with you," Bonnie placed a hand on Nat's knee, "But... well... you're planning to come out on Christmas Eve."

"Christmas Eve Eve," Natalie corrected.

Bonnie continued as if Natalie hadn't said anything. "*And* introduce your first real girlfriend to your brother. And mother. *And* try to keep the peace between them. *And* cook a ridiculously complicated feast that would overwhelm even Martha Stewart. That's a lot."

Natalie stood up. She wasn't going to let Bonnie lecture her.

Since she'd been fired from her job and moved back to

Hagerstown, her whole life had been about restoring this house and rebuilding her family. Those weekly dinners with her mom, while not the Disney-fairytale feel-good solution she'd thought they would be at the outset, were helping the two of them make progress. Getting her brother and his wife to agree to Christmas dinner had been a huge deal to her. She loved this time of year, and for once, she had the opportunity to share it with the people who were supposed to be closest to her.

For her whole life, she hadn't even known she *had* a brother. And now he was about to have a baby, her little niece or nephew. She'd set aside her whole life to come back to the east coast after her grandmother's funeral, and the woman's dying wish had been for the broken Roche family to come together.

Natalie didn't have a career or anything else to focus on at the moment. Why couldn't she focus on this? Wasn't Christmas supposed to be about family and miracles?

She gestured to the half-unpacked pile of grocery bags. "Do you got this? I want to unpack the tree."

Bonnie fell silent, nodded, and watched with a worried look as her girlfriend walked out of the kitchen.

Natalie didn't want to worry about all of the ways Christmas dinner could go wrong. That was counterproductive. Instead, she'd soldier on with making this old house sparkle with holiday magic.

After she gathered up the package from the hall, unpacked its contents and assembled them, she plugged the giant fake fir into the wall and admired her work. It was her very first full-size, pre-lit tree. The recently repainted corner of her Grandma's living room bounced back a halo of warm, white lights.

Perfect, Nat thought, *Now for some color.*

With the red, green, and gold decor, the new paint, and the various improvements Natalie had done on her grandmother's house, it was finally starting to feel like her home. Once again, she thanked her lucky stars that she'd made a handy friend that had been able to help her with the giant project of fixing up the place.

The past few months had had Shawn in a tizzy over making sure Nat's house was ready for the impending winter. Besides the daunting tasks of moving, organizing, dump-running, and yard-sale-ing, there had been several structural improvements she'd needed to make.

Her first gas bill in September had been astronomical. Shawn had suggested switching over her propane furnace for a mini-split, but she'd balked at the initial quote. Then there had been a few problem windows and exterior doors that had needed replacing, roofing tiles that needed patching, and porch supports that needed sprucing. She watched as her renovation budget shrank before her eyes.

As it was, the $125,000 her grandmother had left her was beginning to seem like a much smaller cushion now that Nat had a house to pour it all into. And she was feeling more and more guilty about skimping on Shawn's pay the more time he spent fixing up her house. He refused to accept any money. All he wanted in return was a little help with his online business marketing and the vintage Chevrolet Bel Air that he'd found in Nat's garage that summer.

Oh right. My other Christmas project.

She carried out the cardboard to the detached garage and shivered at the wind that swished through the stark branches of the trees in her backyard. She was grateful that she and Shawn had compromised on the heating system debate by installing some electric baseboard heaters. The living room felt delightfully warm and cozy whenever she returned, carrying boxes labeled **X-MAS DECOR** from the reorganized garage. Eight boxes in all: five from Natalie's former life on the west coast, and three that she'd salvaged from the attic on Thanksgiving.

Bonnie walked in and stood in the archway that connected

the living room with the foyer. She crossed her arms and assessed the tree appreciatively.

"It looks nice." Her lips tilted in a slight smile.

"Just wait until it's got *all* the lights on it." Natalie beamed, opening up a box of vintage bubble lights she was excited to test out. "This whole room is going to sparkle."

"I bet." Bonnie gave a soft laugh, before her face turned serious. "Hey Nat–"

"What are some of your holiday traditions, Bonnie?"

Natalie had her face buried in the box, digging out the antique ornaments she knew were in there somewhere, so she could avoid Bonnie's stare. She wasn't ready to re-hash their conversation from the kitchen. But now that she was decorating again, picking through the vintage lights and baubles she hadn't seen in decades, she realized that the two of them had yet to discuss what Bonnie liked to do for Christmas.

Bonnie walked her way over and kneeled next to the boxes. "Well, first of all, back when I was with my ex, we made a point of decorating the tree *together*."

Natalie looked up at her, surprised. Because Bonnie hadn't mentioned anything about the tree, she'd assumed she wasn't that interested in it. "Oh, I thought..."

"Yeah, I know. I never told you—that was my bad. And I still want to talk about Christmas Dinner." Bonnie's brow smoothed as she lifted a few antique ornaments curiously. Then she met Natalie's eyes. "But this is also *our* first Christmas together, Nat. I don't really have much of a family to spend the holidays with. It's always been my chosen family. My best Christmases have been with just me and my partner, watching cheesy Hallmark movies, exchanging a couple gifts, and ordering Chinese food."

Bonnie reached for her hand. Natalie grabbed it, and squeezed the sensibly manicured fingers. Her heart ached a bit for all that Bonnie had lost when her ex had left her. Was she enough to replace all of that?

"That sounds nice." Natalie coughed through the thickness that had gathered in her throat, "Do you... have any ornaments you'd want to bring over? To hang on *our* tree?"

Bonnie squeezed. "I think I have a couple, actually, if you don't mind?"

"You should bring them over tomorrow night, and we'll do ornaments together. Just the two of us." Natalie smiled. This could be a new tradition, just for them. More than ever, she was convinced that the gift she had hidden in the closet for Bonnie was the right one.

Bonnie smiled and pulled back her hand. "Okay, but we have to make hot chocolate."

"Obviously," Natalie snorted.

"And watch Rudolph."

Natalie laughed, "The Rankin and Bass Rudolph?"

"The *original* Rankin and Bass Rudolph. With the old songs."

The look of absolute seriousness on Bonnie's face spurned Natalie into another fit of laughter. "You didn't strike me as so sentimental!"

Bonnie's face reddened. "It's a *classic*, thank you very much! And, well..." Bonnie fingered one of Nat's grandmother's mercury glass ornaments. Natalie couldn't be certain, but in lights of the tree, it looked like there may have been the beginnings of tears glistening in her eyes. "Once upon a time, when Bonnie was a good little straight-passing honors student at Catholic School... she used to watch Rudolph with her family when they decorated their tree."

She was taken aback at Bonnie's honesty. She still hadn't divulged much about her family. All Natalie knew was that Bonnie's coming out hadn't been on her own terms, and her parents had not been interested in hearing Bonnie's side. She'd been raised Catholic, but didn't go to church anymore (not that Natalie made much of a point of going to church either these days). This was the second puzzle piece of her past that Bonnie had placed on the table in just this one conversation.

Nat was grateful Bonnie was finally sharing with her. She didn't want to mess it up.

"So I don't think I own Rudolph," she confessed, "But I will run to the store first thing tomorrow and buy a copy just for you. For *us*. And tomorrow we will make hot chocolate, gather all the ornaments we care about, and watch Rudolph while we decorate."

"And have nachos?" Bonnie's stomach growled as she asked. "Actually, I think I want nachos tonight—I'm not sure I can wait 'til tomorrow."

"You did get sour cream, right?" Natalie's stomach gave an answering gurgle. When was the last time she'd eaten today? "Because I could absolutely house some homemade nachos with you tonight."

"Yes, and *yes*," Bonnie grinned, reaching across the floor to wrap her arms around her girlfriend. "And Homicide Hunters?"

Natalie nuzzled into Bonnie's neck and planted a kiss on her shoulder blade. "Do they have a Christmas episode?"

She felt Bonnie snort against her hair.

"Only you would want to spoil the respective sanctities of Christmas and Homicide Hunters by insisting we combine the two."

"And only *you* would complain about it by referring to their *'respective sanctities.'*"

"Well, you can take the woman out of the law firm…"

CHAPTER 2

Natalie snuggled into Bonnie's arms when her alarm went off at 6:00 the next morning. She twisted around to face her and gave her a soft kiss on the lips.

"'Morning, sunshine," she murmured.

"Mmm." Bonnie grumbled. It was so funny to her how long it took Bonnie to wake up in the mornings, despite working nine to five for her whole career.

Natalie shuffled out of bed and reached for her phone. The promised winter chill of mid-December was at last beginning to settle into the quiet streets of Hagerstown, and Natalie, for one, was eager to see her first snow since she'd been back. But she still wasn't used to having to check the weather before she got dressed in the morning.

After hunting around in the closet for a loose-knit sweater and some skinny jeans, She went through her checklist for the day. Run to the store for more lights and a copy of Rudolph. Clear out at least another few feet of crap in the garage to unearth Shawn's Christmas present. And finish off the night by putting ornaments on the tree with Bonnie and snuggling with hot chocolate and some claymation reindeer.

She wasn't sure when she and Shawn were going to do their gift exchange (or rather, when *she* was going to gift *him* the antique car that was sitting in her grandma's garage). There were some logistics to work out. She'd love for Shawn to actually be able to take the car home with him, but in order for that to happen, she'd need to hire a tow truck. And she didn't know how to do any of that.

And the person she'd normally ask about it, well... she couldn't, without ruining the surprise.

"It might snow tonight," Bonnie said, snapping Nat out of her planning. She looked behind her at the beautiful woman scrolling through her phone. *How does she look so pretty in the mornings?*

"Really?" Natalie leaned down beside her to see the phone screen. "But how much are they calling for? I can't take another false alarm."

She'd had her hopes dashed at the prospect of snow showers in the forecast twice already since Thanksgiving.

"Supposedly it's going to get pretty cold tonight. They're saying one to three inches." Bonnie frowned. "Do you have snow tires?"

"No...." Natalie winced, "Is that something I need around here?"

She shrugged. "Some people get away without, but it depends on how old your tires are. Is it the same set you drove across the country with?"

Natalie groaned. Since arriving in Maryland, she had hardly had the time to worry about her car, what with all of the legal paperwork and house renovations she'd been worrying about. "Yes?"

"Well then, yeah. You should probably get some."

"O-*kay*," Natalie huffed. "I'll add that to the list of things to do today, I guess."

"Are you okay on funds? Do you need any money?"

Natalie felt her shoulders tense. Bonnie was looking at her with a crease between her eyebrows.

Did she *need* the money? No. Natalie was still living quite comfortably off of her own modest savings and the money her grandmother had left her, even after deciding to split the full inheritance with Ethan.

But the money conversation was beginning to get a little harder for her. Natalie had never depended on a partner to help her put food on the table. She'd been living on her own for twelve years in Los Angeles, eight of those without even a roommate. She knew she'd need to find a job again sooner rather than later, as her savings wouldn't last forever. But Bonnie had her own apartment and expenses to worry about. Even though Bonnie often spent the night and they almost always ate at Nat's house, she never expected Bonnie to pay for anything. Even if, at the moment, she was the only one with a job.

"No, no, I'll be fine."

Maybe I should add job hunting to the list of things to do today, too.

Twenty-nine was too young for a mid-life crisis, yet here she was. She'd worked at the same company for almost a decade. While that might look pretty good to some employers, and she certainly had desirable skills, Hagerstown wasn't exactly the kind of place that boasted gainful employment opportunities. It was mostly a commuter town, with a handful of large local blue-collar businesses. She'd gotten a good deal bartering the car in her garage and some online marketing help with Shawn for his contracting expertise. But other than that, Natalie didn't know of many places around here that could use someone with her skills. It's not like there were any big talent agencies or music venues popping up beside the farmer's market.

"I'm gonna hop in the shower," Bonnie announced, throwing off the covers and rolling up into a seated position. Natalie let herself get distracted by her naked, willowy frame and long, chestnut-brown hair as it cascaded in waves down to the small of her back. She reached over to comb her fingers through the thick, straight locks.

"How come you never wear your hair down?" Natalie crawled into the bed beside her, stroking her hair with one hand and snaking her other arm around her lean waist. Bonnie gave a contented sigh and nestled against her. "It's so pretty."

"It gets caught in everything," Bonnie mumbled, "it's just easier to wear it up."

"Hmm." Natalie twisted a few strands around her fingers and tugged. Bonnie leaned her head back, and she bent willingly into her kiss.

Natalie loved these lazy morning kisses with Bonnie. She knew, without a job, she could get up whenever she wanted, but waking up early allowed her an extra half an hour to savor this gorgeous woman in her bed before she left for the day. She felt a familiar pulsing in her center.

Their kiss deepened, and Nat explored Bonnie's body with her hands: cradling Bonnie's neck, rubbing down her waist, to her slender hips, and twisting slightly so she could reach between her thighs…

Oh yeah. She was horny.

"*Nat,*" Bonnie moaned, "I said I needed to *shower.*"

"But you're still clean," Natalie breathed between kisses, now trailing them down her jaw and into that perfect hollow between her girlfriend's neck and shoulder. "Let me get you dirty first."

"Not fair," she breathed, "I'm the only one naked."

"Mm-hmmm." She kissed her collarbone.

"I can't return the favor."

"Mmm. Mm-hm." A smile curved at the corner of her lips as she licked her way down to Bonnie's breasts. She liked the idea of focusing completely on her girlfriend's pleasure this morning.

"You're–" Bonnie gasped. "Not playing–fair–"

Natalie clamped her mouth around her nipple, and another sweet moan escaped from Bonnie's throat.

"Oh, God, Nat…"

"Lie back down."

"Nat…"

But Bonnie obeyed as Natalie helped hoist her hips back further onto the mattress, cradling her legs against her sides while she continued licking and teasing at Bonnie's modest breasts. She loved the way the dark pink skin around her nipples puffed against her lips, how the peaks hardened as she got hotter. Loved trailing her fingers down the sides of her trim waist. Bonnie was so sexy. And *so* enjoying this.

Natalie knew that if she reached her fingers in between Bonnie's legs right now, she'd be soaking wet.

As if to confirm this, Bonnie moaned again and reached her own fingers toward her panties. Natalie moved to massage her breasts with her hands as she trailed her tongue down toward her belly button and lower, teasing the lace waistband of her thong.

"Don't stop with your hands," Bonnie said, as she grabbed at the lace and shoved her panties down her legs. Natalie shifted to give her space, continuing to knead and flick at her breasts with her fingers. The second Bonnie kicked the fabric away, Natalie returned her mouth to Bonnie's skin, trailing lower. She kissed first at the soft skin at the crease of her hips, then the apex of her thighs, before moving inward to the mounds of her outer lips.

Bonnie groaned, "Yes, Nat, oh *God* yes."

Natalie ran her tongue along the outside of her, just barely grazing her center with her lips. She smiled as her girlfriend bucked a little, and Natalie pulled back to look at her.

This whole time, she'd still been playing with Bonnie's breasts, but now she had other plans for her hands. She found Bonnie's wrists and grabbed them, pushing her hands to her chest to pick up where she'd left off. "Play with yourself."

Heat flashed in Bonnie's eyes. "This is a new side of you I haven't seen," she said, but she obeyed, circling and kneading her fingers around her chest. "What else do you want me to do?"

"Open your legs wider."

Natalie smiled as Bonnie once again executed her instructions, and *damn* was it hot to see her rolling her own nipples between her fingers while she spread apart her legs in the air. Natalie cradled one thigh against her chest and stroked two fingers up and down Bonnie's dewy curls.

She watched as her girlfriend's eyes fluttered closed, and a swallow bobbed down her throat. Her lips parted as Nat switched to her thumb, slowly moving up and down to separate her lower lips. Nat leaned down to kiss her, and as she swirled her tongue inside Bonnie's mouth, she wedged her middle finger into her slit, gently applying a soft pulse of pressure to her opening.

"Oh," Bonnie pleaded, "Yes, Nat, please."

The word had barely left her lips when Natalie pushed inside, with just the one finger at first. She pressed the heel of her palm against Bonnie's clit while she curled her finger again and again inside her.

"Oh! Oh, God," Bonnie jerked, her hands gripping the sheets and her back arching off the bed as her eyes burst open. "Oh, *fuck*, Nat that's–*ohh!*"

"Yes, honey, yes, you just stay right there." Natalie pressed her other hand against Bonnie's stomach and pulled her fingers out of her pussy quickly. Bonnie jerked at the fast movement, and Nat licked her two middle fingers, tasting her arousal briefly before pushing both fingers back inside her and redoubling her efforts, curling and straightening her knuckles faster and faster against the tightening walls. Bonnie arched again, panting, and her eyes widened as she climbed closer and closer to climax.

"Nat! Fuck, I'm gonna–"

"Oh yeah, honey, I want to see you come for me!"

The woman was wriggling against the sheets, her breath coming in pants and her legs shaking with the tremors coursing through her body. *God, she's so beautiful like this.* Natalie remembered how Bonnie had made *her* come like this the very first time they'd had sex, after they'd met at the bar when she'd first arrived in town.

Wetness was soaking Natalie's fingers. She pulled them out and rubbed little circles around Bonnie's clit, making her buck even more wildly.

"Oh God, honey, yes! Yes," Bonnie breathed, her mouth stuck open on a wordless scream. Natalie slowed her fingers slightly, holding her on the edge while she dug in the nightstand with her other hand.

"I know what you need to come, sweetie," she murmured as she grabbed one of her favorite toys from the drawer.

Since they'd started dating, Natalie had seen the value in having a small collection of dildos and vibrators. Back when she'd dated men, she'd enjoyed the feeling of being full during sex—and she'd discovered Bonnie was also a fan of that feeling as they'd explored each other.

She met Bonnie's gaze as she whimpered at Natalie's slow, light fingers teasing her clit. "Please, honey," she begged, and Natalie dragged her tongue along the side of the purple silicone.

"You want this?" She wrapped her lips around it.

"Yessss," Bonnie moaned.

"You want to come all over it?"

"Yes, honey, please..."

Natalie grinned. "Since you asked nicely..."

She tucked the tip of the toy in between Bonnie's slick lips and slid it up and down the length of her slit, soaking it in her juices. Bonnie's back sank into the bed, and she wiggled, attempting to sink it inside of her by tilting her hips.

"Ah-ah-ah–play with yourself." Natalie enjoyed watching her squirm.

"Nat–"

She stopped rubbing and pulled the toy away. "Play with your tits, Bonnie. Or you don't get to come."

Bonnie whined, but grabbed her small breasts with both hands, pinching at the swollen skin there. Her nipples poked out hard, and Natalie's throat made a little noise.

Now *she* was starting to soak through her panties.

"Good girl." She plunged the dildo inside of her, and stroked faster against her clit. In seconds, Bonnie was shaking again. Little whimpers turned into louder and louder cries, until–

"Honey! Honey! I'm coming! Oh–"

Her whole body shuddered and her hands left her chest and reached toward Nat, grasping at her forearms as she shook through her orgasm. Her eyes squeezed closed, and her fingers gripped Nat so tight she worried she'd have bruises. Natalie switched from her fingers to her palm as she applied firm pressure against Bonnie's mound. She slowly came down, grinding against Nat and the dildo as her breathing returned to normal. At last, she opened her eyes and gave her girlfriend a satisfied smile.

"Oh man, honey. That was pretty hot, you ordering me around like that."

"Yeah?" Natalie shot her a naught grin. "You liked that?"

"Mm-hmm." She relaxed her legs open and Natalie slowly

pulled the toy out of her, then leaned down to give her a long, lingering kiss.

She climbed off of the bed to get to the bathroom, waving the toy. "Just let me wash this off before you get in the shower."

Bonnie chuckled. "Take your time. I'm gonna need a minute."

CHAPTER 3

*B*onnie took an extra few minutes in the shower, even though she knew she was cutting it close. But the warm water felt so good as it eased the muscles in her back, lulling her into an even cozier buzz than the orgasm had by itself.

She loved mornings at the farmhouse with Natalie. Sure, the water smelled a little sulfury this far out in the country, and the house itself was still a little dated, but waking up next to that beautiful woman made it all worth it. She loved how Natalie's warm, squishy body felt against her when she was the big spoon at night, and she could run her fingertips up and down the length of her side, until eventually her arm got too heavy to move anymore and she let it sink into Natalie's soft waist. She loved how playful she was in bed, constantly surprising her like she did this morning. If given the opportunity, she'd spend hours kissing and cuddling with her in the afterglow.

But she had to rinse off and get dressed for the day. She still had five more days of work at the law firm before she could clock out for her Christmas vacation: ten glorious days of no research, paperwork, or contracts, that she could spend all alone with her perfect beautiful girlfriend.

Even when she'd been dating Christel, she'd never been able to spend all of the holidays with her. Like Natalie, Christel had still been in the closet to her parents, and despite them dating eight years she'd never told them about her.

She supposed she should have seen that as a portent of their eventual break-up. Christel had been steeped in the political machine of D.C. (in the office of a prominent Republican senator, even), and never would have given up her career for something as silly as love.

For a time, their secret relationship had been enough for Bonnie. Until she'd realized that they'd always be hiding.

So they'd broken up, and Bonnie had finished up her ten years working in the public sector to have her student loans forgiven, and accepted a much better-paying position at the Law Offices of Sheffield and Yang, over an hour away from the I-95 beltway and all the stress of D.C. She'd just established herself as partner when Natalie had walked into her life.

For the first few months they dated, they hadn't shared their relationship with too many people. They hadn't even wanted to admit it to themselves. With Bonnie overseeing the family inheritance battle and Natalie losing her job, there hadn't been a real opportunity for them to explore their relationship, but in the end they hadn't been able to deny their chemistry. Between the amazing sex and their cozy weekend dates in which Bonnie re-introduced Natalie to the east coast, they'd fallen into a comfortable routine.

Their first holiday together, Thanksgiving, had been quiet; instead of jumping into a big family get-together with her still-new relatives, Natalie had asked if Bonnie would want to spend it with just the two of them. The week before, Natalie had insisted they each pick their favorite side dish to make (green bean casserole for Nat, mashed potatoes with gravy for Bonnie).

They'd roasted a chicken and cooked together at the farmhouse, shared a bottle of wine, and finished off the evening with some Tarantino movies.

She couldn't remember ever having a more perfect holiday.

But as Natalie had gotten more settled, and she and her friend Shawn had done more improvements on her house, she had wanted to establish her life beyond just her romantic relationship. Particularly, her family life. She told Bonnie the morning after Thanksgiving that she wanted to introduce her to her mom and brother.

While she was grateful that Natalie didn't seem intent on hiding their relationship from her family, she did worry about her timing. Nat was already freaking out a little bit about Christmas dinner being perfect. After all, it was the first time she was having any of her family over to see the house since all of her renovations. Was it really the best occasion to come out to her mom and brother and introduce Bonnie as her girlfriend?

She turned off the water and quickly got dressed. It was her nature to assume and prepare for the worst in big family moments. She'd spent a decade in family court, after all, and had seen enough custody battles, inheritance appeals, and divorce settlements to convince her that every family had problems.

But that doesn't have to mean they're all broken beyond hope, she corrected herself. Just because she hadn't heard from her parents in the twenty years since she'd come out didn't mean that Natalie's mom and brother wouldn't be accepting of *her* sexuality.

Her heart squeezed when she came down the stairs and saw the plate of eggs and a perfectly toasted bagel on the edge of the table, next to a hot cup of coffee with just the right amount of milk in it.

"This is amazing, Nat. Thank you." Bonnie glanced at the

clock on the microwave before sitting down. "I think I have enough time to eat."

"Do you have to be there that early? It's only 7:30."

"I got a text from Lacey saying there's a partners' meeting at nine. Which means I have to get my paperwork for my 10:00 in order before that. Plus, I usually pick up donuts for all of us."

Natalie snorted into her coffee. "You don't *have* to pick up donuts. I'm sure Steve or Andy are capable of feeding themselves."

Bonnie raised an eyebrow as she scooped some egg onto her bagel and took a bite. Her partners at the law firm were *probably* able to feed themselves, but they were less cranky when she brought them snacks. The runny yolk oozed onto her fingers as she savored the delicious breakfast Nat had made. "You'd be sher-prizhed," she said through the mouthful, holding her hand over her mouth to avoid spraying crumbs.

Natalie chuckled into her coffee. "Sadly, I don't think I would. I used to work for the poster-child of 'adult toddlers'."

Bonnie nodded, and swallowed. She remembered how stressed Natalie had been when they'd first met. Her job (and more specifically, her boss) had been a nightmare throughout the whole inheritance debacle. "Why is it always up to the women to take care of everything?"

"Right? After all the years working for Seth and needy rock-stars, I honestly couldn't believe it when I finally met a decent man. And around here, of all places. I had all but lost hope."

"You mean Shawn?" Bonnie tore off a chunk of bagel and dragged it through the yolk on her plate.

Nat nodded. "He's a good egg. Still an idiot sometimes, but like, in a lovable way, you know?"

Bonnie chewed thoughtfully. She honestly wasn't sure if Shawn *was* as good a guy as he seemed, or if he just bent over backwards for Natalie because he was head-over-heels for her. A fact that Nat was somehow oblivious to.

Her hesitance to agree with her girlfriend gave her pause. Was she jealous of Shawn? *No, that's not right...*

She was grateful that Natalie had a friend around here she could trust, even more so that he had helped convince Natalie to stay on the east coast. But given how often he was over here, she was sure that her girlfriend spent more time with him than herself most days. And yet, for some reason, Nat had chosen to date Bonnie over Shawn the sexy handyman.

Well, sexy for a guy, she supposed. She wondered sometimes if Natalie saw him that way. But she didn't want to assume her bisexual girlfriend was secretly pining after Shawn. Something about that didn't sit right.

"He's pretty alright, I guess." She washed down another bite, swallowing her misgivings with a swig of coffee. "This is delicious, by the way. Thank you so much for cooking. Want me to pick up something for dinner?"

"We're doing Mexican, aren't we? Nachos and Rudolph?"

"Oh, right." Bonnie had forgotten they'd agreed on nachos. She was looking forward to a quiet night of tree decorating and takeout with just the two of them. In all the planning for the dinner and the last-minute home improvements that Natalie and Shawn had been scrambling to get together before the holidays, she'd been missing their alone time. "I need to get my ornaments and stuff for that..."

Natalie stood and kissed Bonnie on the forehead. "I can pick up dinner, if you can't."

Bonnie looked up. Natalie had already turned around to refill her mug. She was pretty sure that Nat already had a full roster of things to do today.

"No, no, I can do it! It just might be a little later."

"Bons," Natalie shot her a look. "It's okay. You've got work, and it sounds like it isn't slowing down at all. Plus, you need to pick up your ornaments. I can get us dinner."

"Are you sure?"

Bonnie's chest tightened. Natalie had been so sweet all morning: cooking breakfast, offering to pick up dinner, initiating sex... while *she* was questioning her feelings for her best friend and leaving early to buy donuts for a boring meeting with a bunch of ungrateful dudes.

Natalie's hands came down on Bonnie's shoulders, her strong fingers rubbing into her muscles. She couldn't help a soft moan that escaped her throat as her girlfriend kneaded into her neck. *That feels amazing...*

"I am really excited about decorating the tree together. So the sooner you can get here, the better. Besides," Natalie rubbed down Bonnie's arms and leaned in to whisper in her ear, "I want plenty of time to finish what we started this morning."

Bonnie's stomach warmed at the thought of returning the favor she'd been paid. She pictured Natalie being the one squirming on the bed instead... "Oh?"

"Mm-hmm."

The weight on her shoulders lifted, and then Natalie was filling up a travel tumbler with the last of the coffee. She handed it to Bonnie after once again pouring in the perfect amount of milk, and kissed her cheek.

"Have a good day at work today, hon. I'm gonna warm up the car."

"Thanks, Nat. Love you."

"Love you too."

Bonnie watched her grab her keys and bounce out the door. Then she grabbed her briefcase and suit jacket, slipped on her heels, and headed to work.

CHAPTER 4

"*E*xcuse me, do you have the *original* Rudolph?"

Natalie hated asking for help. But she'd been studying the end-cap displays of holiday DVDs for the past twenty minutes trying to pin down one copy of the original Rankin and Bass Rudolph the Red-Nosed Reindeer. So far, the closest thing she could find was some weird animated direct-to-DVD sequel that boasted "12 New Songs!" and "Special Never-Before-Seen Bonus Scenes," none of which actually came from the nostalgic television special she was looking for.

But Bonnie had specified that she wanted the original version, with the old songs. And she wanted to prove to Bonnie that she could give her *everything* she asked for.

Her cheeks flushed at the memory of their morning exploits, when the harried-looking employee lifted their tired eyes up to hers. "You have to buy the Collector's Edition box set for that, ma'am."

Natalie glanced up at the top shelf of the cardboard display case, where the "Christmas Classics Collector's Edition" boasted its contents.

"Twenty of your favorite holiday classics," she read aloud from the back of the case, scanning the list. While she saw a screenshot of the claymation Rudolph on the back, the title itself wasn't listed. She was skeptical. "It doesn't say it includes Rudolph."

"It's in the *'and more,'*" they grunted.

Natalie wasn't convinced, but she'd already used up all of her people skills for the day on this limited interaction. She smiled. "Thanks."

She carried the DVD over to another aisle and, once she was sure she was out of view of the employee, dug out her phone to check to see if the box set actually included the original Rudolph.

It didn't.

"Dammit!" Natalie hissed, setting the box set on a shelf of Barbie dolls and trying to escape the store without them catching her leaving without it. She hated leaving it in the wrong aisle, but the thought of bumping into the employee again while returning it after specifically asking for help gave her anxiety. She knew she was probably overthinking things; the store packed full of stay-at-home moms and grandparents rushing to finish up their last-minute Christmas shopping. It was pure pandemonium.

Instantly, she felt sorry for the store employees who had to deal with the chaos of all the pre-Christmas shoppers. The shelf before her was an absolute train-wreck; no semblance of intended organization remained from the onslaught of rowdy shoppers. She froze in the aisle, waffling back and forth in her mind before finally carrying the DVD back to the holiday movie end cap display where she'd picked it up. The same employee was still there, re-arranging the boxes. In the exact spot she needed to be to put it back.

"Um..." *God.* She hated being awkward. "I've decided against it."

They barely looked at her as they straightened shelf after shelf. "Kay. You can set it anywhere. I'll get to it."

"Oh! Okay. Um." She perched it on top of the corner of the bin filled with holiday pillows beside them. "Thank you for your service!"

I am such an idiot. She was surprised fire didn't erupt from the soles of her shoes with how quickly she speed-walked out of there.

Once safely in her car, she took out her phone and googled *where to buy original–*

"Rudolph the Red-Nosed Reindeer" was the first autocomplete answer to pop up, and she felt justified in her frustration. She clicked on it. The results weren't promising.

"Uggggh I seriously need to order it *online?*" Natalie thunked her forehead on the steering wheel. Then her phone buzzed.

> **SHAWN FROM MCDS**
> When are we hanging lights again?

Natalie smiled.

> **ME**
> Tomorrow, if you're still free!

> For my best client? I'm always free 😊

She felt a twinge in her gut. Some client she was, when he refused to accept payment for anything. *I really need to get that car in order.*

> Great! I'll see you at 9am sharp then! I'll have coffee and breakfast ready 😊

Flipping back to Google, her heart sank a little more with each swipe of the page. The only original copies of Rudolph the Red-Nosed Reindeer seemed to be VHS copies from individual sellers on eBay, which would take days to arrive. She checked the time. She was going to be late for her appointment at the Tire and Lube.

In the waiting room, Natalie scrolled endlessly through seller's pages trying to find someone within overnight-shipping range that didn't cost a fortune when her phone rang.

"Mom!" Natalie chirped, "How are you?"

"Busy, busy, busy!" Her mom sang through the phone.

Michelle Roche was a workaholic. Some things hadn't changed since her parent's divorce almost twenty years ago, and that was one of them. While Natalie's mother's official job title was "accountant," she'd been so steeped in the finances of K Street that she had a hand in just about all the goings-on in D.C. and a hefty stock portfolio. Despite that, Michelle refused to retire. Instead, she took it upon herself to use her extra money to invest. Specifically, she liked to invest in restaurants: the kinds of creative, up-and-coming places with personality chefs, where she could bring her clients for fancy luncheons and flex her entrepreneurial spirit.

"I wanted to call about the menu for dinner this weekend," Michelle continued, "Rafael is allergic to peanuts."

"Rafael?"

"My date. I've told you about Rafael before, haven't I? The one who was in *Wine and Table* magazine?"

Natalie blinked. She had mentioned Rafael once or twice, but only when she was talking about her latest investments. He was the head chef of a Latin-American fusion restaurant Michelle had recently taken under her patronage. According to several impressive articles she'd shared over their weekly dinners, he was one of Michelin's "40 Chefs Under 40 to Watch" south of New York City. But this was the first Nat was hearing of any *relationship* between them.

"You and Rafael are *dating?*"

"Is that so surprising?" She heard her mother sigh. "You

know, just because I'm an older woman doesn't mean young, talented men can't find me attractive, Natalie."

"Mom, that's not what I meant. It's just..." *Huh. What* did *she mean?*

"It's just?"

There was a pause while Natalie considered her words carefully. She and her mom were on better terms than they had once been, but the truce they'd navigated was a delicate one.

"I just... um. I had planned for a smaller dinner, that's all. I may need to rethink the menu..."

"With no peanuts. And it's just one extra person. Surely it isn't that much trouble?"

"Right. No, no, it's fine." Natalie pinched her nose. *There goes the peanut butter cream pie.* "No peanuts."

"Perfect." The sound of her mother typing echoed across the line. "What are you up to today?"

Finding another dessert to make for the five–no, six of us. "Getting snow tires put on."

"Smart. They're calling for a storm tomorrow night." Michelle's voice had the polite, but rushed tone of someone trying to speed through a conversation with a business associate. She was in work mode, and Natalie was likely one of the line items on her checklist.

"So I hear."

"Well, I'll leave you to it. Looking forward to Saturday night, darling. *Ciao!*"

"Love you mom."

"Mm-bye."

The click of the line resonated in Nat's ear, and she closed her eyes. So her mom was dating a chef.

A young chef.

A young, Brazilian, borderline-celebrity chef, who was literally on her payroll.

Natalie sighed. She wanted to be happy for her mother, but

she couldn't help but see something a little hypocritical in her dating Rafael. Granted, she knew that love could be complicated. But her mother was the same woman who had held a 20-year grudge against her father for having dated Ethan's mother.

Ethan's mother, Adrianna, had dated their father, Gregory Roche, in high school, years before he and Michelle had met. They'd broken up when he'd left for college, and he'd never known that Adrianna had gotten pregnant with Ethan while they'd been together. Greg found out years later, and even though he and Michelle had since gotten married and had Natalie, he insisted on sending Adrianna money to help care for Ethan, his son. Problem was, he'd never told Michelle about it. It was the unearthing of that secret that spurned their divorce.

Even now, years later, Michelle spoke of Adrianna with venom in her voice. And Natalie had suspected it wasn't just the secret baby that contributed to her mother's ire.

Natalie didn't know the whole story, but given the fact that Ethan's last name was "Espinoza," and that Michelle had seemed especially dismissive of the fact that Adrianna had worked as a janitor at the same college where Greg had taught, Natalie had assumed that race had played a role in her mother's opinion of Adrianna.

It didn't help that many of Michelle's clients were senators that held rather public views on immigration policy, few of which could be considered open-minded.

Now, Michelle herself was dating someone who'd immigrated here and, intentionally or not, had kept it secret from Natalie. Under other circumstances, Natalie would be happy to hear that her mother was dating again—and to find out that she wasn't as bigoted as she'd assumed.

But when it interfered with the plans of her perfect Christmas family dinner...

Nerves bubbled in her stomach. Now she was starting to understand why Bonnie had been concerned about inviting her mom to join her half-brother and his wife. What would *Ethan* think of her mother's new boyfriend? How would Michelle handle being around Ethan and Clara? How would all of them react to Bonnie being there? Or the fact that she and Natalie were dating?

And what would Natalie make for dessert if she couldn't make peanut butter cream pie??

When she'd first planned a quiet pre-Christmas dinner with just Ethan and Clara, she'd been excited to make it part of their Christmas tradition. Now, the logistics were beginning to eat at her.

With a shake of her head, she decided to ignore the family drama. She couldn't control any of the emotional reactions of her family members or their partners. All she could do was welcome them into her home and feed them delicious food (that they weren't allergic to), and just be the best version of herself she could be.

She clapped her hands on the steering wheel and switched focus to the one thing she *could* control: the menu. For the third time that day, she turned to Google, typing, "unconventional desserts to serve at Christmas dinner."

"Oh now *that* could be fun..." she murmured at the first result, and opened her notes app to copy the ingredients to her grocery list.

CHAPTER 5

Bonnie Baker typed out the last sentence of her final email of the day, leaning back in her leather office chair and breathing out a sigh.

"Lacey, I'm done for the day," she called, pressing the intercom button on her phone.

"You got it, Ms. Baker."

She shot off a quick text to Natalie to let her know she was on her way to pick up her Christmas ornaments, then started packing up her briefcase.

For the first time in a while, she was actually starting to feel a little of the Christmas spirit. Of course, when she was around Natalie, who's Christmas spirit positively oozed from every pore, she seemed like a grinch in comparison. She usually didn't get too excited about the holidays.

It's warranted, Bonnie thought. After all, the past two Christmases she'd spent alone. Two years ago, she'd been newly single just as all the storefronts had begun to put out all their decorations. And last year, she'd been entirely alone in her new apartment from Christmas Eve through New Years. In Bonnie's mind, the cheer and the music and the spirit of the holidays that tried to shove its way down her throat at every intersection was like a punch in the stomach.

Look, Bonnie, at how joyful and happy the world is! While you wallow in despair!

Sleigh bells ringing and snow glistening hadn't felt to her like a winter wonderland. It had felt like a bad omen.

Her cell rang with a phone call. She smiled, seeing her girlfriend's name, and pushed the bad memories from her mind.

"Hey, Nat, I'm just–"

"Hey Bons, change of plans," Natalie interrupted in a haze of noise. It was difficult for Bonnie to make out all the words. "I had to run to the grocery store and test out a new recipe for this weekend."

"What?" Bonnie plugged her opposite ear, hoping that it might help her understand better. It didn't. "Nat, it's super noisy over there, what are you doing?"

"Sorry! Sorry." A small crash, and then the background noise ceased. "Is that better?"

"Yes, thank you. What was that?"

"Grandma's old Kitchenaid... I think the motor might be going on it." Natalie answered.

Bonnie shook her head, finally processing all that Natalie had said earlier now the cacophony in the background had settled down. Natalie was baking. She had gone to the grocery store, and... "Wait—you're changing the menu for this weekend?"

"Yeah, turns out mom's boyfriend has a peanut allergy."

"You mom's boyfriend?" Bonnie blanched.

"Yeah, don't get me started on that. Anyway, I've never made a meringue before but it looks pretty simple on *The Great British Baking Show*, and I found this recipe for a pumpkin spice baked alaska–"

"Nat, since when do you attempt to make meringue??"

In the time that they'd been dating, Natalie had exhibited a fair degree of skill in the kitchen. But ham-fried rice and chicken sausage chili were a far cry from the mile-long list of intricate dishes Natalie had planned for this weekend's Christmas dinner, most of which would be intimidating for even the most seasoned chef. Bonnie was pretty sure adding even more to her plate, including *baked alaska* of all things, wasn't going to end well.

"The recipe said it's intermediate difficulty; I can handle that." The sound of the mixer clunked and churned in the background once again as Natalie talked over it. "Also, I couldn't find Rudolph in the store today. I did order a copy, though, so I was hoping we could just postpone tree decorating 'til it comes in? You're still welcome to come over, of course."

Bonnie fingered the clasp on her briefcase. Oh, boy. Natalie was spiraling. This dinner had been an awful idea at the outset, and now it was only getting worse. Michelle was bringing a boyfriend? Nat was already changing the menu? What other disasters would pop up between now and Saturday to drive her girlfriend over the edge?

Bonnie remembered the last time Natalie was in over her head: two weeks before she'd ended up getting let go from her job. She had completely shut everyone out, and when the building chaos had inevitably imploded at the last minute, Bonnie had been useless to help her.

She wouldn't let that happen this time around.

But Natalie had doubled down every time Bonnie had tried to convince her to pare down on the Christmas festivities. How could she voice her concerns to Natalie without sending her deeper down the rabbit hole? How could she make sure she actually supported her, instead of doubting her? It was a dangerous tightrope to tread.

"Would you still *like* for me to come over?" Maybe she could read ingredients to her, or something. Or find an easier dessert they could make together, so it wasn't all on Nat's shoulders.

There was a pause on the other end of the line, broken up only by the sound of the mixer cutting in and out.

"I mean, I guess you don't have to, if you don't want to." The confusion in Natalie's voice told Bonnie that that *hadn't* been the right thing to say. She'd completely misunderstood what Bonnie intended.

"I always *want* to come over." She said in a rush. "I just don't want to be in the way. It sounds like you're dealing with a lot over there. What if we found a different dessert together that was a little simpler?"

"Ummm..." Natalie drew out the word in a way that made Bonnie feel like she was only half listening. "The oven timer just went off, Bons. Look, I can handle this recipe, okay? Let's just hang out tomorrow night instead."

"Oh." *Dammit.* She was retreating again. *What do I do?* "Um. Sure, Natalie. I love you."

"Love you too."

The words sounded like a reflex. The line stayed open for a few seconds as the sounds of Nat in her kitchen ambled on, until Bonnie finally tapped to end the call.

Should I go over there anyway?

The question weighed heavy as Bonnie drove back to her apartment to find the box of ornaments she'd been planning to bring over. As she rifled through the hall closet, memories of all her past Christmases washed over her.

As a kid, of course, she'd loved the holidays. What kid didn't? Presents, pie, and a week off from school—what's not to love?

But when the teachers at Catholic school had discovered the notes she and another girl had been passing in math class and told her parents she was queer, she'd been kicked out of her parent's house. Every day was a struggle after that. And the holidays had come to represent more of what she *didn't* have: family. Traditions.

She had been able to rely on the generosity of queer charities and friends' families for a while, transferring to public school and redoubling her focus on studies to get into a decent college. Her friends in undergrad and law school that had similarly complicated relationships with the holidays had thrown Friendsgivings and hosted smaller, casual get-togethers to ring in the many new years, but Christmas itself had always been a rather lonely affair. Her ex had been the first person to really build a tradition of a quiet Christmas evening with Bonnie... after she'd already visited with her parents and family for their big luncheon and gift exchange. Bonnie was never invited to those particular celebrations.

Despite also living alone for most of her adulthood, Natalie seemed to have all sorts of Christmas spirit. Her house was absolutely packed with decorations, and she'd shipped a literal dozen boxes of lights and decor from her storage unit in California when she'd moved here in the fall. She'd told Bonnie that, after having grown up with fairly stark Christmases with just her and her mom, she'd gone all out on fostering the holiday spirit once she was on her own. The storefronts, festive seasonal menus at chain cafes, and elaborate office holiday parties out west helped her feel the spirit, even if Natalie didn't have anyone to share it with.

But now, she did. A half-brother she was hell-bent on reconciling with, for some reason; a frosty mother with an unexpected boyfriend; and, of course, Bonnie.

But Bonnie felt she was beginning to get lost in all the window dressing. Natalie was panicking so much about dinner: the menu, the guests, and everything else, that she'd canceled their tree decorating.

Bonnie didn't really care all that much about Rudolph, but she *did* want the chance to start some intimate Christmas traditions with her girlfriend, without having to compete with Natalie's complicated family.

No, she thought, chastising herself. *That's not fair. You'll get to* have Christmas with just the two of you once this dinner is over. Let her have this.

Once she dug out the box of ornaments, she sent Natalie a text.

> **ME**
> Hey hon, how about I bring over breakfast for us in the morning? And I can come over right after work, too.

> **NATALIE**
> 👍

> And send me pics of the meringue when the prototype is done!

There. That was supportive. Right?

When there was no response, Bonnie set the ornaments box by the front door and went to fix herself a frozen dinner.

THE NEXT MORNING, Bonnie tossed the covers off with purpose, shivering a little in the winter chill that had settled in her bedroom overnight. It had been a while since she'd woken up without another body to keep her warm. She and Nat had been spending the night with each other since Halloween.

Last night hadn't been ideal, that much was clear. But while she'd been heating up her Lean Cuisine, Bonnie had developed a plan: Operation Supportive Girlfriend. Natalie was clearly in over her head with Saturday's Christmas dinner, and even though Bonnie wasn't *officially* on holiday vacation until Friday night, she could still contribute by making sure Natalie didn't have to worry about any other meals that week.

An hour ahead of her usual schedule, she was up and out the door: which turned out to be a blessing. The snow that they'd been calling for had finally materialized. A solid three inches of the stuff covered Bonnie's car along a thin layer of ice that, while pretty to look at, added an element of danger to her trek down her porch steps.

It also added to the amount of time it took her to clear off the car.

Twenty minutes later, defroster blasting, she was on her way to pick up donuts and coffee from their favorite weekend spot downtown. The owner smiled at her from the counter when the bells rang above Bonnie's head.

"Another early meeting?" She greeted her.

"No, actually–this one is for pleasure, not business." She scanned the menu board for their seasonal holiday flavors. "Can I get two Boston Cremes, a cafe at lait, and a Sugar Plum latte to go?"

"You got it."

Natalie loved her super sweet flavored coffee drinks. She had confessed to Bonnie, when pumpkin spice season had started that year, that latte flavors had been one of the ways she'd kept track of time passing in Southern California, where there was really only one season: summer.

Bonnie had picked on her a bit for it (especially since she usually drank her coffee black or with just a little milk), but since they'd been dating she'd loosened up a bit on the frilly cafe drinks. She hoped her girlfriend would appreciate the gesture.

A minute later, Bonnie was balancing the drinks tray back to her car to make her way to Natalie's house. Her heels slid a little in the icy parking lot; the sun had risen fully and begun to just slightly melt the icy patches underfoot.

A chilly fog had settled in the valley. As she wove through the mountains, her car trekked between serene, sunny landscapes sparkling with fresh snow and foggy, forested passes still shaded by the Appalachian peaks. At last, she flicked her signal to turn into Natalie's skinny country driveway, but was forced to skid into the breaks.

It was blocked. By an old white pickup truck.

What on Earth is Shawn doing here so early?

A glance in the bed of his truck on her precarious route to the front door gave her her answer. Piles of extension cords and strings of lights were thrown into the back, as well as a few giant bags of road salt.

When she walked around the pickup, Shawn's goofy grin greeted her. He had a shovel in his hand, and a rough path of the gravelly drive was cleared behind him.

"Hey, Bonnie!" He waved, then gestured to the drink carrier in her hands. "Any of that for me?"

She grimaced, before twisting her face into something that she hoped would pass for an apologetic smile. "Hey Shawn. No, I'm sorry, I didn't realize you were coming over this morning."

At least, I hope you came over this morning...

Natalie hadn't called him for his help last night, had she?

"Well, I wasn't supposed to be over 'til later, but I remembered Nat didn't have any salt or nothin' for her sidewalk so I figured two birds, you know?"

She didn't find his cheerful country kindness reassuring. She knew why he was here, being all helpful. He was here to steal her girlfriend.

Well. He could keep trying. *She* had donuts and coffee to deliver. She shot him a deceptively cheerful smile.

"Nat inside?"

"Yep–in the shower."

How the hell did he know that??

He began to whistle as he continued shoveling the drive, and Bonnie walked around him and into the freshly cleared path, trying to ignore the needles of insecurity that poked at her. It was fine that Shawn was here. Shawn was practically always here, after all, and he and Natalie hadn't gotten up to anything in all that time. She had nothing to worry about.

"Nat, I brought coffee!" Bonnie called as she walked into the foyer. The slightly sulfury smell of the well water drifted down from upstairs, and Natalie shouted down from the source of the mist.

"Be right there!"

She walked on to the kitchen and set the tray and the bag of donuts on the table. Mixing bowls toppled over in the sink, no doubt the carnage from last night's panic baking, and the counter was still coated in a sprinkling of powdered sugar.

Oh, Nat. And she had just cleaned the place.

Knowing that they'd probably both want another cup before she left for work (and, begrudgingly, that Shawn would want some), Bonnie dumped grounds in the coffee maker and started brewing up a pot. She shrugged off her coat, dug an apron out of one of the drawers to cover up her work clothes, rolled up her sleeves, and started washing the dishes.

By the time Natalie made it down the stairs, she'd cleared out one side of the sink.

"Bonnie! You don't have to do that!" She had bundled up her curvy frame in a pair of baggy jeans, a black turtleneck, a ratty Smashing Pumpkins World Tour t-shirt that she'd tied into a knot around her hips, and a bright red paisley bandana that she'd used to pull her hair from her face like a headband.

She was adorable.

"Well aren't you the little country farm girl?" Bonnie smiled at her, and patted her hands dry with a dish towel. She shrugged twards the sink. "It's the least I can do. How'd the dessert turn out last night?"

"Ugh," Natalie groaned, reaching straight for the donuts. "The meringue turned out like rubber and the ice cream melted all over the place. I ended up having to wipe out the oven and by the time I got all that cleaned up it was after midnight."

She yawned, and shoved the donut into her mouth. The little moan of pleasure she made sent a shiver down Bonnie's spine. *No, Bons–focus.* Supportive *girlfriend mode, not horny mode.*

"Oh no! You poor thing!"

"Yeah, sho I godda fih-ger tha' out," she chewed. She eyed the coffee cups, squinting at the writing on the side. "Does that say Sugar Plum Latte?"

Bonnie grinned at her. "It sure does."

"You're the best." She grabbed the coffee and sniffed at it appreciatively. "Where's Shawn?"

"Shoveling." Bonnie shrugged. The happy, slightly horny glow she'd been feeling dimmed a bit.

"That dude..." Natalie shook her head. "What did I do to deserve such great people in my life?"

"You're pretty great yourself, you know." She slipped the apron off and pushed away from the sink, pulling Natalie into her arms as she wound them around her waist. "And I gotta say, I'm kinda digging this butch-grunge, Rosie-the-Riveter thing you got going on."

"Haha, yeah?" Nat set her coffee down and shoved the last bite of donut into her mouth, then leaned into Bonnie's hold. She twirled her fingers through the wisps of hair at the nape of her neck, eyes hooded and cheeks puffed out like a chipmunk until she finished chewing and said, "It's no sexy lawyer..."

"Eh, sexy lawyer's overrated." Bonnie's chest felt warm as she took in the sweet, round face of her girlfriend. "But the bandana's really doing it for me."

Their faces were closer now, and Bonnie could feel Natalie's nose scrunch in a grin against her cheek. She kissed at the soft skin along the crest of her jaw, planting little smooches in a line across her face.

When their lips met, she could taste the traces of chocolate glaze at the corners of her mouth. Slowly, she nipped at her plush bottom lip, savoring her for a second, before–

The screen door slammed open and a gust of chill air blew through the foyer back to where they were standing. Bonnie jumped, and Natalie chuckled, planting another quick peck before they pulled away from each other.

"Oh. Didn't mean to interrupt…" Shawn muttered as he stomped his snowy boots into the room. He set a 5-gallon paint bucket of stuff down by the pantry and left a trail of little puddles behind him when he crossed to the counter to pour himself a cup of coffee.

"You weren't interrupting," Natalie said. "Bonnie's probably got to head to the firm soon anyway, right?"

Bonnie blinked, still a little warm from the Natalie's embrace. She checked the clock.

Damn. She was right. "Yeah. You're right. What's your plan for the day?"

"We gotta sweep off the gutters so we can hang the lights." Shawn grabbed one of the spoons Bonnie had just washed from the drying rack to stir creamer into his coffee. "Right, Nat?"

"Yeaaah, I guess we do…" Natalie rolled her eyes and shoved her hands into the pockets of her jeans. "Jeez, I thought the first snow of the year would be fun and pretty. Turns out it's just annoying."

Bonnie and Shawn both laughed at that, and then they looked at each other. Shawn's mouth quirked at her in a half smile, and Bonnie returned it. *Well,* she thought, *I guess that's one thing we can agree on.* The heavy, icy snow of a Mid-Atlantic winter really did lose it's charm once you were out of grade school. Natalie had left for the west coast before she'd had to deal with the consequences of an overnight snowfall as an adult. But Shawn and Bonnie both understood the struggle.

"Thank you again for the coffee, hon. I'll see you tonight?" Natalie pushed onto her tip-toes to kiss Bonnie's cheek.

"Absolutely."

Shawn interrupted then, refocusing the couple on the tasks at hand.

"Hey Nat, I brought you a little something extra for the decorations…"

There wasn't another goodbye kiss in the shuffle of winter

coats and to-go cups, with Shawn and Natalie discussing the logistics of their days' mission. Bonnie just gave a slight wave as she slipped out the door, which was met with only a distracted nod from Nat. She tried not to take that too personally as she headed to her chilly car.

CHAPTER 6

"*A* little to the left!" Natalie called out to Shawn from across the front lawn.

Yep. The whole "White Christmas" charm she'd convinced herself she'd missed during the eleven years she'd lived in California was definitely a whole lot more appealing when she wasn't standing in the middle of it. Her knuckles were chapped beneath her cheap polyester gloves, her toes were soaked in her wet sneakers, and she had to blow hot air into her hands to warm them up, which only served to add to her overall feeling of *damp* and *cold* once she pulled them away from her mouth.

"Here?" Shawn called back from the ladder, sliding the scalloping of the colored lights two inches to the left.

It still wasn't even.

"Split the difference?"

"Ah, Nat, come on, no one's lookin' that close!" He fidgeted with the hammer at his hip and dug a finishing nail out of his pocket. "We've been out here for hours!"

He wasn't wrong. With the exception of a couple hour break for a delivery pizza lunch, they'd been outside all day stringing

Christmas lights through just about every inch of Natalie's property.

But it certainly looked merry and bright now. Especially the porch. The squidgy, splintering deck boards of the front stoop stairs had been the first thing Shawn had replaced that summer, back when the two of them had made their bet that he could help her fall in love with the little farmhouse. And now, three months later, it was still her favorite feature of her new home.

She and Shawn had positively plastered it with every kind of light and Christmas decoration they'd sold at the surplus outlet she'd raided the week before: icicle lights dangled from the overhang, light-up candy canes obscured the supports of the railing; even a giant, animatronic Santa sat in the rocking chair beside the door and came to life and greeted everyone who walked by. And of course, after being greeted, all visitors would wipe their boots on the festive doormat, which read "There's some HO'S in this house."

She thought Bonnie would get a kick out of that one.

"Alright, alright, you're right. Get it all secured and come on down, then."

The *bang bang bang* of his hammer echoed across the valley. Natalie crunched over to the ladder and held onto the legs to support him on his way down.

Just then, Bonnie's sedan wheeled up to the hedgerow in front. She emerged with takeout bags with the signature sombrero'd emblem of José's Crab Shack, their favorite Mid-Atlantic-Mexican fusion place, and a bottle of wine she must have picked up from the liquor store. Natalie cursed under her breath.

The Rudolph VHS still hadn't come in, and she'd forgotten (again) that they were supposed to watch it while they decorated the tree that night.

"Shit! Shawn. *Shawn,*" she hissed, trying to keep her voice low enough as not to alert Bonnie, who was already approaching the door. "Did you ever find that copy of Rudolph in your parent's Christmas stuff?"

"What?" He yelled down around a nail between his teeth.

Bonnie stepped closer. Too close. "Nevermind," she muttered.

Shawn banged another nail in place, and Bonnie winced as she made her way up the sidewalk.

"Still working?" Her eyebrows raised, and she looked like she was holding back a grimace. "I thought you'd be done with lights by now."

"We are!" Shawn hollered, as he hooked the wire on the final nail. He leaned back to admire his work. "I think we're ready to plug these in, Nat!"

"I can grab it," Bonnie said, setting down the food and wine on the stoop and reaching for the extension cord bundled behind some of the outdoor furniture. "This one right here?"

She plugged in the bright orange cord into the new outside outlet that Shawn had installed by the front door. Instantly, the house lit up in a flash of a thousand tiny bulbs. Unfortunately, Santa also came to life in the rocking chair, raising his arms and shouting, *"Ho, Ho, Ho—Meeeeerry Christmas!"*

Bonnie leapt back from her crouch by the rocker, tripping over the step and knocking the wine and the takeout bags to the sidewalk below. Natalie jerked in surprise, yanking on the ladder a bit, where Shawn had also jumped slightly at Santa's outburst. And as he'd already been leaning back to check the lights, that extra momentum from his and Natalie's reactions sent his body careening in a free-fall toward the ground.

"Nat!" He shouted, and she looked up just in time to see his skinny ass falling right toward her face.

Her only reaction was to hold out her arms fruitlessly, despite the fact that there was no way she was strong enough to break his fall in any way that wouldn't end in disaster.

He crashed on top of her, and they both fell back into the

hard-packed snow beneath them. Black and magenta spots danced in her vision as the wind was knocked out of her, and she couldn't find the breath to ask what that crunching sound was as the world turned upside-down.

"Nat! Honey, are you okay??" Bonnie crawled over to her on her hands and knees at the same time Shawn jumped off of her and scrambled to his feet.

"Nat are you alright?"

She gaped like a fish at them, unable to get her lungs and voicebox to cooperate.

"We gotta call an ambulance."

"An ambulance? Naw, give her a second, she probably just got the wind knocked out of her. Nat? Can ya hear me? How many fingers am I holding up?"

Shawn waved a hand in her face with his pinky and thumb tucked in. She blinked, still gaping, and held up three of her own fingers.

"See? She'll be okay. Just give her a minute."

"Jesus Christ, Shawn, she is *not* okay!"

And suddenly, her lungs started working again. She took in a shuddering, gloriously cold breath, and swallowed, before attempting slowly to sit up.

Pain shot through her arm when she planted her palm on the frozen grass.

"Owwww ow ow!" She winced, rolling to her side.

"Honey!"

Bonnie crouched over her, concern etched into the perfect little lines on her forehead. Natalie counted them. *One, two, three...*

"Hon, are you okay? What hurts?"

"Four..."

Bonnie glared at Shawn. "See? She's got a concussion."

"No, no, it's my wrist. I think I just sprained it." She leaned on her other arm, which seemed okay, to prop herself up. Her back protested, but other than that she seemed okay. "Luckily, Shawn's a scrawny little thing."

"Hey!"

But the relief on his face belied any offense in his tone. He was clearly glad to see that Natalie had found her voice again.

"Let me see." Bonnie held out her hand, and Nat placed her wrist in it. The lawyer clucked as she gently rotated it left and right, gauging her girlfriend's reaction. After the third quick exhale of breath, Bonnie patted the air above the injury and pursed her lips. "Alright. We're running you to Urgent Care. It's starting to swell."

"But you brought wine!" Natalie whined.

"Pretty sure the ground drank it all," Shawn said sheepishly, toeing the shards of glass scattered across the landing.

So that was the crunching noise I heard earlier.

Bonnie looked up at Shawn. "Can you get her to the car while I clean up?"

"I can clean up."

"Oh, Shawn," Natalie shook her head a bit too fast, and the many bright lights swam in her vision. She stopped. "You don't have to do that…"

Bonnie's lips were set in a thin line as she scowled at Natalie. She nodded her head to Shawn. "Thank you. That would be really helpful, actually."

"Don't mention it."

Natalie tried not to groan as her girlfriend helped her to her feet and towards the driveway. "You've got a key right?"

Shawn winked at her. "O' course I do. Don't worry, this'll all be cleaned up when you get back."

She paused, and Bonnie turned to look at her. Natalie hung her head for a brief moment, before taking a deep breath and muttering, "Can you unplug Santa so he doesn't scare us when we do?"

He laughed, and even Bonnie's stern expression cracked into

a reluctant grin. She shook her head, and slowly led her to the car.

"Come on, Vixen. Let's get you patched up."

CHAPTER 7

Bonnie flipped impatiently through a July issue of *Southern Living* in the waiting room of the Hagerstown Urgent Care. Natalie was back with the second shift PA, and she had a sneaking suspicion that she'd likely be coming back with a prescription for a couple of braces and instructions to take it easy.

Instructions that Natalie Roche would almost certainly do her best to ignore.

Her phone buzzed, and she rolled her eyes at the incoming message.

MR. FIX-IT
How's our girl?

"Our" girl. Annoyance bubbled in her stomach at that, and as if in response, it let out a little growl. Although, that could just be hunger. After all, the she-crab nachos she'd picked up from Jose's Crab Shack were currently feeding the colony of ants that lived in between the cracks of Natalie's sidewalk. Along with the expensive bottle of Pinot she'd picked up to celebrate their new holiday tradition.

Hunger, annoyance, and regret. These were the feelings that fought for dominance as she skimmed a recipe for *Red, White, and Blueberry Jello Salad* and debated how she wanted to respond to Shawn.

> ME
> Still in the exam room. We'll let you know.

Should she have called out his use of the word "our"? She wondered if picking a fight with him was counterproductive to Operation Supportive Girlfriend.

"Are you waiting for someone?"

A tall black woman in neon floral scrubs pointed at her with a pen in the window.

"Not a doctor–just my girlfriend. We think she sprained her wrist, and maybe an ankle?"

"The shorty with the big ass?"

Bonnie laughed, and rose from her chair. "That's the one."

Natalie wasn't all that much shorter than her, if she were being honest, but being 5'5" in three-inch pumps and a power suit made Bonnie a much more imposing presence than her wide-hipped, 5'4" girlfriend in boyfriend jeans and Vans.

"She'll be out in a second. What happened?"

The husky-voiced woman looked down her nose at Bonnie with the curious expression of a woman with a taste for tea. She walked over and leaned against the laminate reception counter to read her name tag: *LaDawna*.

"What else? A man."

"Figures." LaDawna put her pen down across her stack of papers, upon which Bonnie could make out a Sudoku puzzle. The woman crossed her very muscular arms and nodded her head to a pamphlet rack beside the check-in. "Forms for domestic abuse–"

"Oh, no, no, he didn't hit her," Bonnie corrected quickly. "I'm sorry, that came out really wrong. She was holding the ladder for a friend of ours while he was hanging Christmas lights, and he fell on top of her when the porch Santa shouted at him..."

She trailed off. LaDawna's eyes widened, and then she leaned her chin on her hand.

"Oh, this I gotta hear."

"I don't even know the whole story," Bonnie admitted, adding "guilt" to the cocktail of emotions swirling in her empty stomach.

"Make somethin' up. I still got 50 minutes left of my shift."

Bonnie was about halfway through explaining Natalie's obsession with Christmas decorations and the story of how they'd driven home from the surplus outlet with the life-size Santa crammed into the back of her Toyota Corolla with his curly white beard streaming out the window, when Natalie emerged from a door leading to the back.

"So we've lost his wire glasses, and she's got me scrambling through her grandma's old desk drawers to find a pair of readers—"

"That is *not* how it happened and you know it!" Natalie cut in, giving Bonnie an extra cranky look as she hobbled over, one crutch under her left arm as she swung her right foot in a walking cast. Her other arm, which was wrapped in a fabric brace, cradled her sneaker against her chest.

"Oh hon," Bonnie looked her up and down, surveying the damage. She took the sneaker from her. "You poor thing."

"That Santa has been more trouble than he was worth from the beginning. I don't care that he was seventy percent off. He's a menace."

"Should I give you a form to fill out to report him? I hear he's responsible for millions of break-ins every Christmas Eve, too." LaDawna offered.

Bonnie was really beginning to like her.

"Form?" Natalie blinked at them both.

"Never mind," she and LaDawna chorused in unison. Then

LaDawna retrieved her pen from the Sudoku book and waved to Natalie. "Lemme check you out, hon."

Conversation turned to business as Natalie swiped her card at the terminal, balking slightly at the fee. Bonnie winced. Thank God Natalie still had a few months left of her COBRA insurance. She couldn't imagine what the bill would have been were she uninsured.

As they walked to the car, she tried to find a diplomatic way to breach the topic.

"What was the damage?"

"A brace, the walking cast, a prescription for ibuprofen, and $300."

$300? "And that's *with* insurance?" Bonnie balked.

"'Tis the season for surprise expenses, I suppose." It took Natalie a few extra moments to navigate the car door and the seatbelt with her plastic boot and crutch. Bonnie cranked the defroster. "I'm starving. Can we grab something on the way home?"

"Sure. Why don't you spend the night at my place? I've got wine there. I'll drop you back off at the house on my way to work. I don't trust that Shawn remembered to unplug Santa." *Oh right.* She was supposed to text him. "Can you shoot him a message to let him know you're alright? He asked how you were doing."

"Such a sweetheart." Bonnie could see Natalie's smile in the blue light of her phone screen out of the corner of her eye. She swallowed down the snarky retort that itched the back of her throat, and turned into the Taco Bell drive-thru.

It wasn't Jose's Crab Shack, but she'd be damned if after all this she wasn't going to have her nachos.

WHEN THEY MADE it to the house that Bonnie rented in town, they'd had to do a little shuffling. Her apartment was on the second floor, and even with the salt that her landlord had sprinkled on the steps, the icy path was slightly treacherous.

She probably should have thought about that before suggesting they spend the night there. Bonnie grabbed Natalie's crutch and held out her arm so she could use her for leverage as they took the stairs one-at-a-time.

Finally, they reached the landing, and exhaustion was clear on Natalie's face. As Bonnie flipped the hall light on in the small landing, she realized with a start its utter lack of festivity when compared to Natalie's home. No Christmas tree in the corner of the living room, no holly wreath on the front door, and (although this was a more positive realization) no six foot tall animatronic Santa to greet them with terrifying well-wishes.

It also lacked the warmth that Natalie had cultivated in the few months she'd lived there. That was one of the more pleasant side effects of Natalie's inability to sit still: her constant drive to improve, impress, and always move forward, meant that there was always a sense of momentum around her. It permeated her home; even in its semi-permanent state of disarray since she'd moved there, it felt optimistic. Like a work-in-progress that just oozed potential from every creaky floorboard.

Bonnie's apartment, on the other hand, was tidy and minimal. She had a cleaner come once a week to help maintain a sense of order. Her kitchen was all white imitation marble laminate and brushed stainless steel, as opposed to the mishmash of new and old appliances of Natalie's house. Bonnie's landlord, an elderly couple that lived downstairs, had renovated the place a few years before Bonnie moved in, and they were happy to have such a low-maintenance renter who kept the place clean.

But as a result of its sparkling cleanliness, it also felt a bit impersonal. Frozen in time. Whereas Natalie's home strove to manifest its potential with its eclectic assortment of odds and ends, Bonnie's was content to sit untouched and pristine like a photo in a furniture catalog.

She let Natalie lean on her as they crossed the vinyl plank floors of the open layout to the slate-and-cream area rug that separated that patch of floor as the living room. She deposited Nat on the matching cream couch, and reached over the simple walnut end table to tug on the lamp pull by her head.

A soft glow illuminated the space. Natalie rocked forward on the squishy cushions to plop the Taco Bell bag on the glass coffee table. She glanced down at the latest editions of *The New Yorker* and *The Economist*, as well as that day's paper, fanned neatly across its top, angled just so beside the wooden basket that held the remotes and a few pens for the morning crossword.

She'd stayed at Bonnie's place before, of course, but lately they'd taken to spending their nights together at the farmhouse. It had just felt more…

Like home.

Bonnie stood for a second, a little lost as she watched her girlfriend gingerly toe off her one remaining sneaker and lean back. Natalie looked over, nodding at the kitchen.

"Are we doing plates and silverware? Or eating off the paper?"

Bonnie snapped out of her daze and walked briskly past the island that separated the kitchen from the rest of the apartment. "The only dishes I'm interested in getting out are some wine glasses. Red or white?"

"Red for me, thanks."

A pang of regret tugged at her stomach for the vintage Pinot she'd picked up for that evening, currently watering the hedges in front of Natalie's porch. She grabbed a cheap cab from the wine rack above the fridge and two glasses, twisted off the screw cap, and poured them each a hefty serving.

"Should we see what's on the TV?"

"Sure," Nat said, already reaching for the remote. A half

smile lifted Bonnie's lips as she punched in the numbers for the Hallmark Channel. *Knew it.*

She set Nat's glass on the end table under the lamp and set her own on the matching table by the other arm of the couch. Then she went about distributing their dinner while Nat elevated her ankle on a pillow.

"How are you feeling?" Bonnie handed over a burrito.

Natalie placed it in her lap, electing to take a swig of wine first. "Stupid."

That wasn't the answer she'd been expecting.

"What? Why?"

Nat thumbed down the volume on the TV and sighed, then unwrapped her burrito. "It's just... I don't know. Maybe you're right. Maybe this whole dinner is a bad idea, and I should just kind of accept it. My family's broken. Mom's selfish. Ethan's got his own whole thing: a wife, a kid on the way, and I'm..." Her shoulders sank. She bit into her burrito and chewed a moment. Bonnie waited, her car-tossed nachos growing soggy in her lap. "I'm butting in where no one actually wants me."

"I never said that."

Nat's eyes drifted to the TV, her gaze unseeing as a slight frown pulled at her face. On the screen, an unrealistically beautiful blonde woman rolled out dough in an industrial kitchen with a silver-haired lady that looked like Sally Field. Suddenly, a dog rushed into the scene and the blonde tripped over the furry blur, slipping on the floor and throwing flour all over the place.

Just as she was about to hit her head, though, another too-attractive actor caught her, a man with light brown hair and sparkling blue eyes. Natalie snorted, took another sip of wine and a giant bite of her burrito. Bonnie looked back at her, and guilt twisted in her stomach. She placed a light hand on her elevated foot.

"I don't think you're stupid."

"Of course you do," Nat said around a mouthful of beans and tortilla. She swallowed. "And you're right. I'm in over my head. *Something* was bound to go wrong. Although I am a little surprised that it ended up being Shawn falling off a ladder and squishing me."

"Yeah, my money was on the meringue catching fire," Bonnie teased.

Nat smacked her.

"Hey, now, I'm joking!" But she caught the laugh that Nat was holding back, twinkling just behind her eyes. Her expression turned thoughtful. Seeing Natalie so defeated robbed her of any relief she may have felt at her admission that she's overcommitted. "Do I think you're in a bit over your head? Sure. But it's not cause you're stupid, honey. It's because you want to see the best in people. Like Ethan. Like your mom."

Natalie had so much faith that her family could come together. Bonnie didn't think it was likely that Christmas dinner would go well, but she also knew that Natalie wouldn't have been trying so hard if it wasn't important to her. She pinched off a soggy clump of nachos and stuffed it in her mouth.

Natalie looked at her. "Do you think they're not worth it?"

Bonnie chewed pensively, wiping her fingers on a napkin and reaching for her wine. "No," she said finally. "It's not that they aren't worth it. It's just...I watch you try so hard to please everyone. Your old boss. Ethan. You want so badly for them to like you, and I just wish you could see that it doesn't matter if they like you. You *are* a likeable person, a *loveable* person. Even if they don't see it. Yet," she added, seeing the crease in Nat's brow as she took in Bonnie's words.

She looked up. "Do you think they ever will?"

Bonnie took in a breath, wine glass tilted to her lips.

No, she thought. But that wasn't fair. Bonnie's opinion of Natalie's family was colored by years of working in family court and her own depressing history. She didn't lack faith in Ethan and Michelle because of who they were, she lacked faith in them because she lacked faith in *people,* period. You could wrap them in whatever shiny gift paper and ribbons or Christmas dinners you wanted; family still sucked.

"I think that, whether or not they do, it's not a reflection on *you.* And you shouldn't feel like it's your responsibility to *make them* see how great you are. You're still great, even if you don't cook an entire Christmas dinner by yourself. I still love you, and I'm still dating you, whether or not your family knows the full extent of our relationship. Having their approval doesn't *make* you worthy of it. You are worthy. With or without their say-so."

God, it felt good to finally say that. Bonnie looked at her girlfriend's face, still wrinkled in thought, as she took in her words. All she wanted to do was reach across the couch and smooth her face of all the worry and self-doubt. She loved this woman. This empathetic, over-achiever who wanted so desperately to repair the family she never knew she had.

She put her nachos on the coffee table and got up off the couch, and Natalie looked up in surprise. "Where are you–?"

Bonnie bent down and swallowed the rest of whatever Natalie was going to say, pressing her lips to hers. She felt Nat's face tense in surprise, only to relax a second later as she returned the kiss. Their lips melted together, and Bonnie teased and tugged at Natalie's bottom lip, pulling it lightly in between her teeth.

Nat's mouth opened a little, and Bonnie took the opportunity to push her tongue inside, exploring slowly, gently. *I love you,* she thought, trying to embed that feeling into every point of contact between their bodies, as she pressed her mouth more firmly against hers. She reached her hand behind Natalie's neck, supporting the cheek that was leaning against the high arm of the soft couch, and trailed her other hand down Natalie's exposed neck, over her t-shirt and down to her waist.

They both gasped, breathing much heavier than they were a

second ago. Bonnie smiled at her, brushing away a few hairs that had fallen out of Natalie's messy bun with her thumb. She pressed another kiss to her temple, holding her mouth against the smooth skin of her forehead, and breathing in the scent of her hair, touched ever-so-slightly by woodsmoke, from her day working outside hanging lights around the chimney.

"I'm so tired, Bonnie." Natalie laughed, and she *did* sound tired. She'd been working so hard, and this had not been the relaxing end to the day that both of them had been anticipating. "The wine is starting to hit me."

"How about I help you get ready for bed then? Starting with getting you out of these clothes…"

Bonnie reached down to her waistband and undid the button on Nat's jeans. Natalie shifted, lifting her leg slightly to make it easier for her, and she put a hand on her thigh. "I got this, Nat. Let me take care of you."

She thought she saw moisture glisten in Natalie's eyes before she blinked it away. "They're pretty heavy legs, there, Bons."

She gave her a look–a slightly sexier version of the one she'd use in the courtroom to quell a bogus objection. "I can manage. I've handled myself around your thighs before."

A blush crept up Natalie's cheeks. *Adorable.* How did she do that? How did she manage to be so cute, even when she was dressed in ratty jeans and an old t-shirt, and had bags under her eyes from running herself ragged for days?

She didn't care. This woman on her couch was perfect. And she was going to make her come at least twice before she finally fell asleep tonight.

Bonnie leaned down and lifted her other leg onto the couch beside her elevated ankle. Carefully, she undid the velcro straps on the plastic boot, peeled it off, then lightly touched Nat's still-socked foot. "Be right back."

Natalie nodded and reached her arm over her head to grab her wine. Bonnie crossed over to the kitchen and grabbed a bag of frozen peas from the freezer. When she returned to the couch, Nat's eyes had drifted closed, and her wine glass was empty and drooping from her hand.

Or maybe she just needs sleep tonight.

She unbuttoned Nat's jeans and slipped them down her hips, doing her best to keep from knocking her ankle around too much as she wiggled them down Natalie's perfectly plump body. Natalie moaned a little, and the sound was so enticing that Bonnie found herself pressing open-mouthed kisses down her legs as she peeled the denim off her calves.

A little sigh escaped Natalie's lips, and when she'd stripped off her pants, placed the bag of peas on the injured ankle, and looked up, her girlfriend was staring at her with hooded eyes.

Was that a look of exhaustion, or lust?

"I could stop here, cover you with a blanket, and let you watch Christmas movies until you fall asleep. Or..."

"Or?" Natalie's voice was gravelly and low.

And sexy as fuck.

"I could yank your panties down and give you a better end to the night."

"Mmm..." Natalie's eyes glinted a bit and Bonnie decided it was definitely lust that shone there. "I like the sound of option two."

"I thought you might." Bonnie returned her uninjured foot back to the floor and knelt beside it, bending to lick her way up the inseam of Natalie's leg. She gasped, and Bonnie's lips curled into a smile. God, she loved how sensitive she was. Instead of pulling off her underwear right away, though, she played at the lace edges with her fingertips, running her nails lightly along the skin underneath, as she planted kisses in a line up her body.

The soft, smooth skin under the lace was *so* tempting. But Bonnie made herself take her time, teasing with small strokes up and down the sensitive skin, until she could hear Natalie's breath catching above her.

"Oh, Bons, you're killing me... that feels so good..."

"Yeah?" Her mouth was inches away from her entrance as she said it, and she felt the woman jerk beneath her when the puff of warn air from her lips teased at her. A little shiver traveled down her body, and goosebumps erupted over her legs.

"Ooh. Yeah."

"Hmm..." Bonnie pulled away, just for a second, to snatch a throw blanket off the back of the couch. She draped it over her arms like a cape and swooped down to cover up Natalie's exposed skin while hiding herself under the soft blanket. In the darkness, she felt once more for the seams of Natalie's panties and tugged them to the side.

She could feel the heat of her as she eased her face closer, licking a line up the slit of her entrance. A slight pressure found Bonnie's shoulder as Natalie put her hand on top of the blanket.

"Oh God, honey—"

Her voice was muffled from under the covers, but Bonnie got the gist. She licked again, and again, tracing the same line in a deliberate rhythm a few times before pulling apart Nat's lips with her fingers and finding the little nub above her opening. It was round and swollen with her arousal, and Bonnie flicked her tongue in little circles around it.

Natalie moaned. Bonnie kept up her pace, pushing a finger in between the slick inner folds under her chin and pulsing a matching rhythm with her knuckles.

The noises Natalie made, accompanied by the little twitches of her legs around her head, made Bonnie's stomach tighten in arousal. After the day Natalie had had, she deserved to feel *good*. And Bonnie could give her that.

She curled her tongue around and around Nat's clit, then pressed her lips in a small *o* around it and sucked greedily.

Nat's thighs jerked up at that, and the hand that had been resting above Bonnie's shoulder on the blanket twisted and gripped at the fabric, snagging some of Bonnie's blouse with it.

She pulled back her neck slightly as she pushed her fingers deeper inside of her girlfriend, curling them in a steady rhythm as she blew cool air on the swollen bud.

A shiver ran up Natalie's whole body. Bonnie loved this. She loved the feel of Natalie, the smell of her. This woman was so soft and inviting and beautiful, and she wanted to make her fall apart, wrap her in her arms, and then fall asleep while holding her. She wanted her to know that she was perfect. She didn't need anyone else's approval. Not her mother or her brother—no one else.

Let me be good enough for you.

She sucked her lips around Natalie's clit once more, pulsing against her inner walls relentlessly. She could feel Nat's body seizing as she approached her climax, her hips bucking into Bonnie's face as she attempted to find purchase with her injured ankle.

"Oh! *Ohhhh*, honey!"

Bonnie lapped up the little gush of arousal that burst from her as her whole body went tight, then lax. She could feel Natalie's thighs relax as her body unwound, her climax unraveling the day's tension. For a moment, Bonnie kept her palm pressed firmly against Nat's center, allowing her to grind it as she rode out the final tremors of her orgasm. When at last she sank into the couch, she slowly withdrew her fingers, tugged the lacy panties back over her, and placed a final kiss on top of the fabric.

She tossed the throw blanket off her head.

"How do you feel?"

Natalie breathed out a tired chuckle. "A little better. Although, I wish I could return–"

"Don't even think about it." Bonnie rose from the couch and tucked the blanket around her, then bent to capture Nat's lips in a kiss. Her girlfriend flinched a little, and Bonnie straightened.

"What's wrong?"

"Just rub it in, kissing me with my cum all over your mouth," Natalie muttered. "If I wasn't so tired…"

Bonnie laughed. "Hey, I'm just returning the favor from yesterday."

Natalie's eyelids were drooping already, but she shook her head slightly. "I want to be good for you."

"Honey…you're kidding, right? You're *so* good for me."

In so many ways. More ways than Bonnie could count.

Natalie was so inspiring to her. Before she'd met Nat, she'd basically given up on doing anything she once dreamed she'd accomplish in her life: getting married, making a difference in the world… she'd been tired and worn down from the cruelty she'd faced. Her ex's betrayal and ten years of working in public service had wrung out every last bit of empathy she had to give.

And then this beautiful woman, whom she had been convinced was some selfish L.A. brat who didn't even care about her own grandmother (and Bonnie's favorite client, Sophie Roche), turned out to be the most generous, hard-working, and surprising woman she'd ever met.

How is it that, after spending half her life in the cut-throat world of entertainment, Nat *still* saw the good in people? And could make people like Bonnie believe in love again?

"You know I love you, right?"

"…loveyew too," Natalie murmured, her head sinking further into the throw pillow as she drifted off.

Bonnie sighed, walking to the kitchen to wash her hands before coming back to the couch to switch out the peas on Natalie's ankle for an actual ice pack. She propped Natalie's wrist in a better position, re-tucked the blanket around her the way she liked, and turned off the lamp. Then, she grabbed a pillow from her bedroom and another blanket from the hall closet.

It's not exactly the snuggles I wanted, but…

She tossed the pillow to the area rug in front of the couch, and curled up on her side, wrapping the extra blanket around herself.

It wasn't the most comfortable solution. But as she drifted off in her makeshift bedroll on the floor, she felt the comforting weight of Natalie's arm flop off the edge of the couch and brush against her hair. Soft snores drifted from above her head, and a relaxed smile smoothed her face.

Worth it.

CHAPTER 8

*A*t 6:30 on Thursday morning, a text came through on Natalie's phone, buzzing loudly on the end table next to her head. *Where am...?*

She opened her eyes blearily, and the bolt of pain that shot up her wrist when she leaned on it reminded her of the events of the previous evening. *Oh, right.*

She was at Bonnie's apartment, and she fell asleep on the couch (which was a little lumpier than she remembered) after Bonnie had once again rocked her fucking world.

She glanced around the living room, wondering if her girlfriend was awake yet. To her surprise, she found her lying on the floor in front of the couch, curled up with a pillow and blanket, despite the fact that her bed was just a few steps away.

A smile tugged at her lips as she let her uninjured hand fall to her girlfriend's scalp and play with her loose hair. She had such pretty long, brown hair, and she always wore it up in a bun. Such a shame.

The movement caused Bonnie to stir, and she groaned as she rolled on to her back.

"Oof. I am not in my twenties anymore," she mumbled,

wiggling a bit as she stretched her back. "I thought I could get away with sleeping on the floor, but…"

"Why did you think that, again?" Natalie teased. Bonnie squinted at her, and Nat handed her her glasses that had been folded on the coffee table.

She unfolded them and pushed them onto her nose, blinking up at Natalie. "How'd *you* sleep?"

"Pretty great, actually. My girlfriend helped me unwind and tucked me in. She's kinda the best."

"Is she prettier than me?"

Natalie lightly slapped her on the cheek. Bonnie's answering chuckle morphed into another groan as she raised herself into a seated position. "I guess I should probably make us some coffee, huh? It's been a while since you've spent the night at my place. I hope I still remember how to use the Keurig."

"Don't you have interns for that kind of thing?"

"They prefer the term paralegals," Bonnie joked.

"Ah."

As Natalie shifted herself to sitting, a thawed ice pack flopped onto the cushion beside her. *So that was what that lumpiness was from.* She checked her phone, where a message from Shawn was waiting for her.

> SHAWN FROM MCDS
>
> Left a surprise for you somewhere in the house.
> Hope you're feeling okay.

A surprise, huh?

Thinking about the kitchen reminded Natalie of the grand plans she'd made for Christmas Eve Eve dinner in two days. The one she'd planned to cook in said kitchen. A task which seemed far more daunting now with a sprained ankle and wrist.

> I've felt better, but the diagnosis is I'll survive.
> Just a couple sprains.

By the time Nat set down her phone, Bonnie was bringing her a steamy mug of black coffee.

"You like it black, right?"

Natalie smiled. She supposed it had been a while since Bonnie had made them coffee. Normally she'd be the one to splurge on something from a cafe, and then she tended to veer toward fun, sweet drinks. Usually, it was Natalie who made them regular coffee in the mornings. "Yes. Thank you."

"You look like you're thinking about something. What's up?" Bonnie perched on the edge of the couch beside her, holding her own mug and looking at her with concern.

Nat sipped pensively before answering. "I'm thinking about what you said last night."

"Yeah?"

"Yeah." She stared into her mug. "I think I have taken on a little too much. Or, at least, I'm realizing I'm not going to be able to do all of the things that I took on. I do think I *could* have handled it before Shawn fell on me. But now, well. I'm going to need some help."

"You could cancel, you know. It's understandable. You got hurt."

The two women shared a look, and Natalie bit her lip at the sympathy in Bonnie's eyes. She knew she probably *should* cancel. Bonnie likely wanted her to. The two of them had said as much the night before.

But she didn't want to cancel. She still loved the idea of a magical Christmas dinner with Bonnie and her brother and sister-in-law, even Michelle and her boyfriend. Was it unrealistic to think that she could bring her family together with the power of Christmas? That one dinner would have them exchanging hugs and hot cocoa, sharing stories from the many years they'd missed?

Sure. One could say that.

But just because it was a little unrealistic, did that mean that Natalie couldn't hope it might *start* to heal the hurt between them all? Did it mean she couldn't try?

"I know I probably should," Natalie admitted, breaking eye contact as she took a deep breath. "But I don't *want* to. I just..." She sighed. Bonnie tilted her head, a slight frown on her lips. But she didn't look like she was upset—more like she was confused.

Of course, it shouldn't surprise her that Bonnie didn't really understand. With the exception of the morning she'd broken down after getting fired at the Stag's Head, Natalie had yet to really talk about her grandmother's dying wishes with Bonnie. The truth was, since she'd moved back to Hagerstown after so many years away, seeing the constant reminders of her grandmother in every corner of her new home, she'd felt more and more like she owed it to Sophie Roche to help mend the family her father had broken. She'd left the house to Natalie with the hopes that she could build a better family than Sophie had. She'd said so in her letter.

She knew deep down it wasn't her fault that her parents had split. She understood that she couldn't have conceivably known she even had a half-brother all those years, let alone reach out to him.

And now that she was an adult, she could see how deeply the hurt ran: in her mother, who even after all these years couldn't say her father's name without it sounding like a curse; in Ethan whenever they inadvertently brought up something to do with the fraught inheritance battle. How could she even begin to express that, by agreeing to live in her grandmother's house, she felt like she'd also agreed to trying to fulfill her wishes? That, somehow, she needed to do this to atone? For leaving all those years ago, and never looking back?

She tried again.

"In Sophie's will, she mentioned that she wanted Ethan and I to try to rebuild our family. And I think she was right to say something. We should try. I'm about to have a little niece or nephew, and I might never have kids of my own, you know? Wouldn't it be better, if we could all actually be in each other's lives? Be a real family?"

"What about your mom?" Bonnie asked, placing a hand on Nat's thigh. "I understand you and Ethan wanting to get along, but do you really think your mom will ever see him as anything other than the kid your dad kept secret from her?"

"I don't know." Natalie stared at a spot on the area rug, her mind too scattered with memories and thoughts of loyalty to really see the situation clearly. "But... I feel like if they *could* set aside their preconceptions, it could only be for me. Because I'd asked them to." She sighed, then changed tactics. "Besides, it's Thursday. Isn't that a little late to just... call it off?"

Bonnie's brow furrowed a bit, and she took a couple sips of coffee before she said anything. Natalie broke off her stare to look at her, a little anxious that her practical girlfriend would try to convince her it wasn't worth it. That she was being a starry-eyed optimist again, and she was only going to get hurt.

"This is what you really want?" She asked finally.

Natalie blinked. "Yes!"

She may have sounded a little too enthusiastic when she said it. Bonnie closed her eyes and nodded ever so slightly, before facing her with resolution. "Alright. Tell me what you need me to do."

CHAPTER 9

"You're not whipping fast enough, honey. You really gotta whisk the crap out of it."

Bonnie bit back an angry retort as Natalie criticized her baking technique once again. *You're doing this to make her happy,* she reminded herself, *to honor Sophie's memory and help your girlfriend have a family Christmas miracle.*

Although the real Christmas miracle would be getting through this dinner without wringing her girlfriend's neck. She should have known that she was signing up for a cross between Kitchen Nightmares and the Great British Baking Show when she agreed to be Nat's sous chef and make her family dinner everything she'd ever dreamed it could be. Natalie was a perfectionist, after all.

The fact that she holds you to the same high standards as she does herself is a good *thing, Bons. It's a sign of trust.*

Trust in Bonnie's patience.

Her arm was about to fall off. When she'd agreed to making the pumpkin spice baked alaska that Nat insisted was the only dessert that could possibly impress her mother's professional chef boyfriend (who was allergic to peanuts, and by extension,

Natalie's tried-and-true dessert recipe: the much easier-to-make peanut butter crème pie), she hadn't realized that the antique Kitchenaid she'd heard Nat using over their phone conversation a few nights ago had shit the bed.

So now she was whipping an Italian meringue by hand. And for the love of God, would these eggs ever fucking thicken up??

"I know you're quicker with your wrists than that," Natalie teased.

Bonnie scowled at her, still whisking. "If I was interested in making things firmer with my hands, Nat, I'd date men."

Natalie chuckled, shifting the bag of frozen corn on her propped ankle. She was taking up two chairs in her grandma's old kitchen, and despite Saturday still being two days away, Natalie had insisted on practicing the more difficult dishes she'd planned since her first experimental bake had failed. Hence why she was directing Bonnie on how to whisk egg whites on the Thursday night before Christmas instead of ordering Jose's Crab Shack and watching Rudolph together.

"You're doing great. I'll check on the ice cream."

Luckily, Nat had had the foresight to make enough of the pumpkin ice cream to fill four of the desserts in advance, so Bonnie hadn't had to prepare that. Just scoop and shape it into a bowl to form the base of the domed dessert.

Bonnie had never actually had baked alaska. And if she had known just how involved it was, she would have never let Natalie talk her into it. The idea of *baking* a dome of ice cream, even if it was covered in meringue, seemed incredibly counter-intuitive. Supposedly, it was supposed to insulate the ice cream from the heat during the baking process. And yet, when Natalie had made it last, it had melted in the oven.

"So I think I know what I did wrong last time," Nat said, gingerly balancing on her good foot while she pulled the cling wrap-lined bowl out of the freezer.

"What's that?" Bonnie switched hands. She was going to give herself carpal tunnel.

"I got too fancy with the piping, and there were holes in my meringue."

"Did you say *piping*?" Bonnie would've gaped at her, but the little flecks of raw egg that kept splashing up with her movements kept her inclined to keep her mouth closed.

"Yeah. How do you think you cover the ice cream?"

"With a spatula."

Natalie's jaw dropped. "You'd serve a dessert to a professional chef with a *spatula-spread meringue??*"

Bonnie slapped the bowl on the table and let go of the whisk. "Nat, this is family dinner, not Top Chef."

"It's *Christmas* dinner," Nat challenged. "I'm breaking out grandma's china for this, Bonnie, this is not the time for a sloppy–"

"Who said anything about sloppy?" Bonnie interrupted. "Just because I don't want to break out a pastry bag–"

"We're piping the meringue, Bons." Natalie had now grabbed her crutch and crossed to the counter, setting down the ice cream and putting her braced hand on her hip.

The two of them stared at each other, and Bonnie's eyes flickered from the stubborn set of Nat's jaw, to the way she leaned her weight awkwardly on the crutch under her arm. The sight of the brace and the boot softened her resolve.

It's her Christmas present, Bonnie. She just wants a perfect family dinner. It'll be over in two days.

"Fine." She snatched the whisk back up. "But seriously, how long is this supposed to take? I've been at this for twenty minutes."

"Did you add the cream of tartar?"

"Cream of what?"

Natalie pointed to the tiny shaker set out in front of the

spice rack. "Tartar. You were supposed to add half a teaspoon. It helps to stabilize it."

Bonnie grabbed it and shook out a generous sprinkle of what looked like cornstarch over the bowl of froth.

Within seconds of more whisking, the mixture began to thicken.

"There you go, see? I'll make a chef outta you yet."

Bonnie rolled her eyes. "Don't you dare. For Valentine's Day, you're getting a frozen Sara Lee cheesecake simply out of spite."

Natalie shot her a toothy grin. "Hey, if we're still together for Valentine's Day after I'm making you do all this, then I'll consider this dinner a success."

A nervous cough of a laugh bubbled from Bonnie's throat. She supposed she should take it as a good sign that Natalie felt comfortable enough with their relationship to make that joke. But the idea of them splitting up over this dinner made it even harder for her to commit to the idea of helping Natalie pull it off.

Miraculously, the meringue did thicken to soft peaks, and Bonnie was able to flip the ice cream onto the cake round and pipe rosettes of the stuff around the dome neatly enough to gain Natalie's approval. The few minutes they waited for the dessert to bake they spent by snacking on chips and a rejected cheese dip Natalie had tested out the previous week, along with a bottle of Chardonnay.

Thirty seconds before the oven timer was set to go off, Natalie couldn't wait any longer. She asked Bonnie to check the oven.

"Oh no," Bonnie moaned after she'd turned on the oven light.

While the dome of meringue was beautifully intact and carmelized, its peak had sunk slightly, the cause evident in the bubbling lake of orange-tinted cream that coated the baking sheet below the ring of cake.

"Did it melt again??" Natalie hobbled over, hinging at the waist to peek into the oven. She groaned when she caught sight of the ruined dessert. "Nooooo, that should have worked!"

Bonnie tapped off the oven, then carefully slid the cake off of the rack. Luckily, none of the ice cream had spilled over the edge of the sheet pan they'd used for fear of this very outcome. "Any ideas what we did wrong?"

Natalie googled it on her phone. As she studied reference photos, Bonnie poked a fork into the lump of wet cake.

"Mm. It is delicious, though," she said. Natalie ignored her, frowning over her phone screen. Bonnie took one more timid bite and (regretfully) dumped the rest of the contents of the tray into the trash.

"Did you make the meringue thicker at the top? And pipe to cover the sides of the cake layer, too?" Nat asked her, scowl lines forming in her forehead as she squinted at her recipe.

"Umm..." Bonnie tried to remember where the line of piping had stopped. "I think so?"

"Did it look like this?" Natalie twisted the screen to face her.

Bonnie blinked, then adjusted her glasses. Maybe she'd had more wine than she'd realized. The image on the phone didn't look all that different from what she'd done. But then again, she'd never *done* anything like this before. Maybe she'd missed something.

"I don't know, Nat. I'm tired. Do we try again tomorrow?"

The injured woman tossed her phone on the floor and scrubbed her face with her hands. "I don't get it, Bons! We followed the recipe... Do you think it's wrong?"

"The recipe? Or the entire concept of baking a hemisphere of ice cream coated in egg whites? Because even though it might taste good, I'm not convinced the science is sound."

Natalie glared at her, and Bonnie could instantly see she'd hurt her feelings. She regretted being so candid. She was only here because she'd promised she would help her with

Christmas dinner, and now here she was, undermining her plans.

"What I mean is," Bonnie tried again, "Maybe this isn't the right recipe for Saturday. Because there could be any number of things that are wrong. What if we try something simpler? Like pumpkin pie?"

It was a perfectly good suggestion, she thought. But Natalie apparently had other ideas.

"Sure. And mom will just spend the entire dinner complaining about the fact that if Rafael had been the one cooking, we'd have something fresh and innovative, instead of the same, plebeian dessert that's served at every American holiday function." She scowled at her phone, not meeting Bonnie's eyes.

"You really think she'd say *plebeian?*" Bonnie teased, trying to lighten the mood.

It didn't work. "Let's move on to something different. How do you feel about the casseroles?"

And for the rest of the night, Natalie wouldn't hear another word about dessert.

CHAPTER 10

Natalie laid face-up under the covers, staring at the ceiling, and tried to avoid turning to her side for the thirtieth time that night. Bonnie was curled up facing the wall beside her, snoring lightly.

She shifted a little every time Natalie moved, and she desperately didn't want to wake her. Because if she woke her up, she'd ask why she couldn't sleep. And if she gave an honest answer, there would be a fight, and Natalie really couldn't handle that right now.

She had enough on her plate.

The thing was, she knew Bonnie had a point about the dinner. She'd done this to herself, after all: inviting her brother and sister-in-law over and insisting that she could cook for all of them, letting her mom steamroll over her plans, and then pushing herself too far by hanging a million decorations that scared her to death and landed her with an injury that necessitated she ask someone else for help.

And if there was anything Natalie hated, it was asking for help.

The more Natalie ruminated, the more guilty she felt for

recruiting Bonnie in all of this. The entire week, she'd only been preparing for Saturday's dinner. Because of that, the two of them had yet to form their own traditions or hang their own ornaments on the tree like they'd talked about.

Part of that was due to the fact that the copy of the original Rudolph she'd ordered from eBay had yet to come in. *Overnight shipping my ass.* But that wasn't really an excuse; Bonnie would understand if she just told her. Instead, she'd been avoiding the topic entirely, refusing to admit that she wasn't able to acquire the one thing Bonnie had wanted for Christmas and worried that if she did, she'd be admitting defeat to the whole pyramid of tasks she'd assigned herself for the holiday.

So now she was wasting more time trying to impress her biological family than she was being grateful for her found family: Bonnie and Shawn.

I wonder how Shawn is doing?

She hadn't heard much from him since he'd cleaned up from decorating Wednesday night. She still hadn't found the surprise he'd texted about. They'd only texted back and forth a couple messages since she'd ended up in crutches, including one that said his family might have a copy of the OG Red-Nosed Reindeer she could borrow. She should check in with him again.

And figure out how I'm going to give him that car in my garage.

Her head pounded. She had so much to do. As quietly and smoothly as she could with her injuries, she snuck out from under the covers and made her way across the hall to her bathroom. She didn't bother turning on the overhead light. A small Candy-Cane air freshener and nightlight was plugged into the outlet by the sink, and illuminated the space with a soft red glow. After doing her business, she washed her hands and opened up the medicine cabinet to dig out a few ibuprofen.

A pair of glistening, beady eyes stared back at her, and she jumped back, losing her grip on her crutch and landing hard on her bad ankle.

"Ow!" She yelped, stumbling over the edge of the tub and crashing ass-first into the shower curtain. The crutch clattered uselessly to the floor in front of her, and pain shot from her tailbone all the way down to her foot.

The crash broke the late-night silence of the country farmhouse, and Bonnie shouted from the bedroom, "Who's there??"

"It's just me!" Natalie shouted from her heap in the tub, every joint and muscle throbbing. "But there's something in the medicine cabinet!"

She heard some shuffling from across the hall, and then Bonnie crept into the bathroom without her glasses on, wearing nothing but a pair of old volleyball shorts and clutching a rolled up legal folder like a Louisville Slugger.

The picture of her half-blind girlfriend stumbling into the bathroom, tits out, primed to strike, was almost funny enough to make her forget the demon eyes that had caused her to fall in the first place. Bonnie flicked on the light switch, and they both looked toward the medicine cabinet.

An Elf-on-the-Shelf smiled tantalizingly back at them, its creepy expression mocking them from its perch by the Q-Tips.

"Goddammit, Shawn!" Natalie rocked herself into a manageable position before crawling back onto her feet. "Fuck you and your surprises!"

Bonnie squinted at the garish stuffed toy maker before grabbing it. As she did, a note fluttered down to the floor. Natalie snatched it.

Thought you of all people would appreciate a new tradition: hide the Elf-on-the-Shelf!
Merry Christmas, Shawn

She wanted to strangle him.

Bonnie lowered her legal folder and blinked blearily at Natalie. "So, you're safe? Are you okay? Do you need a hand?"

"Yeah, one second." She grabbed hold of Bonnie's arm and she helped her to her feet. Once she was properly balanced, she plucked the Elf and the folder from Bonnie's hands and set them on the toilet lid. Then she wrapped her arms around Bonnie's waist. "Thank you for coming to my rescue."

She wanted to say she was sorry for everything she was putting her through: for making her take on Christmas dinner all on her own, for relying on her too much, for failing to make enough time for her...a million thoughts and excuses barreled through her head, and she didn't know how to express any of them.

But looking at Bonnie, half-naked, in the bathroom light, with messy hair and a bewildered expression on her face, all she could think to say was, "I love you so much."

A soft smile stretched Bonnie's lips, and she leaned in to hug her back. "I love you too, honey," she murmured into her hair. "I'm gonna go back to sleep."

"Okay. I'll be right there."

Natalie watched Bonnie's perfect ass as she shuffled back to the bedroom, then bent down to grab her crutch. She filled a little cup from the tap with some water. After a few sips, a couple pain pills, and one more glare at the evil-looking Elf, she returned to her bed to see if she could actually quiet her mind enough to fall asleep.

But before she curled up next to Bonnie, she sent a quick text to Shawn.

ME

You are such an asshole 🎄😈

CHAPTER 11

When Bonnie walked down the narrow stairs down to Natalie's kitchen the next morning, she was surprised to see her with her crutch, swinging herself around the counters and attempting to make breakfast.

"Nat! What are you doing?"

Natalie had the good sense to look guilty as she limped over with a mug of coffee. "I wanted to make you something to apologize for getting a little testy last night. You're doing your best to help me, and I was being an asshole. I'm sorry."

Bonnie's mouth opened slightly as she took the offered coffee. "But your ankle—"

"It's really not that bad." At that moment, Natalie turned to head back to the counter and whacked her foot against the table leg. She bit back a groan.

"It will be if you don't rest it and keep whacking it on things!" Bonnie set her coffee down and reached for her, easing her into a chair. *I swear, she isn't making Operation Supportive Girlfriend very easy on me.*

She got her settled in a chair. After a few quick steps to the counter and back, she had the bagels Nat had toasted shmeared with cream cheese and served to the table. "Seriously, hon. The best way to thank me for all of this is just to actually rest a little, okay? You've been losing your beans trying to get this dinner together. You need to stop."

"Losing my beans?"

Bonnie glared at her. "You know what I mean. This thing is driving you crazy."

"It's not driving me crazy! Look, I hardly slept last night and now my ankle hurts. I don't need a lecture, okay? I just thought I could handle breakfast, but apparently I can't even do *that* right anymore."

Bonnie sighed, trying to backpedal the conversation. She didn't want to fight before work. "Nat, you're taking on too much with this. It's stressing us both out. Maybe we should–"

"I told you I'm not canceling," Nat warned.

"I know! Otherwise, I wouldn't have spent four hours last night whisking." Bonnie shook her head, frustrated that she'd just assumed that was what she was going to say. She took a second to grab two ice packs from the freezer and calm down, placing one on Nat's propped ankle, and the other on the table for her wrist.

"You know icing after the first day doesn't do anything, right?" Her tone had shifted into something more polite. Despite her words, she rested her wrist on the ice pack anyway.

Bonnie bit back a mean retort. "It helps with swelling."

"Initial swelling, yeah." Natalie took a bite of her bagel. "Bu' shuppozhedly, i' shlowzh healing after. You wanna elevate thuh injury and yoozh heat to increash bloodflow."

Bonnie humphed. Once again, Nat was trying to change the subject. Which meant she knew she'd hurt Bonnie's feelings, but wasn't ready to apologize.

She sat down in her chair and started eating her breakfast without another word.

In general, Bonnie wasn't a fan of the silent treatment.

However, she knew from her years of working with clients that, when someone knew they were in the wrong, the best thing to do was let them talk themselves into admitting it.

She wasn't going to completely ignore Natalie. But she also wasn't going to argue with her when she knew in her heart that Natalie was completely aware of how impossible her expectations were for Christmas dinner.

Something had to give. And it wasn't going to be Bonnie.

"You still think I should cancel, don't you?"

Natalie tried to catch her eyes. Bonnie stared stubbornly at her plate. "I didn't say that."

"Well you clearly don't want to cook everything."

Bonnie flinched, stung a little. Now it was her time to avoid the truth. "I didn't say that either."

What she wanted was for Natalie to dial back her expectations. She was right; Bonnie didn't want to cook everything. She'd spent half the night whisking a dessert that ended in disaster. She also knew she wasn't as good a cook as Natalie even on her best day, and she doubted her ability to handle this dinner on her own. Especially after their fight the night before.

"What else can I do, Bonnie? Ask everyone else to cook because I hurt myself hanging Christmas lights? They already barely like me. The whole point of all of this was to win them over and start a new Christmas tradition. If I ask *them* to bring dinner, then no one will want to come next year!"

Natalie said all this very quickly. So quickly, that Bonnie didn't even really have a chance to dissect it all before she launched into another monologue.

"I mean, maybe I could ask Shawn to help, but he's got his own family he spends the holidays with. And then there's *his* Christmas present–I wanted to get him that car before the end of the month! He's already done so much for me, and I'm nothing but a drain on him. So really the only person I can turn to is *you*, and you're..." She took a breath, and Bonnie's forehead wrinkled.

Where exactly was *that* about to go?

"Good lord. I'm just ruining Christmas for everyone, aren't I?" Tears began to trail down Natalie's cheeks, and Bonnie couldn't stay quiet anymore. She pushed aside her concerns.

"Honey, *no*. No one thinks that." She reached out her hand across the table to grab the one that wasn't sitting on the ice pack. "If you're afraid to ask someone for help because you think they won't like you anymore, then they're not people who's opinion should bother you."

"Huh?" Natalie scrunched her face in confusion. Bonnie tried to rephrase.

"Look. You're a good person, okay? I know you are. Friends and family should love you and care about you because you're *you*. Not because you bake them fancy desserts or decorate your house within an inch of its life." Natalie rolled her eyes at that, but Bonnie continued. "If they hate you because you set boundaries, then you shouldn't care what they think about you. Do you really think Ethan hates you that much? After how generous you've been since coming back? If he doesn't know by now that you're a good person, then he's not worth your effort, honey."

Natalie considered that for a second. "Well, what do *you* think about him? You've seen more of him than I have. Isn't he, like, the town official, or something? Don't people like him?"

Bonnie sighed. The fact that Ethan was so connected in local government was part of what had made settling the Roche estate such a headache in the first place. He wasn't just another client, he was a County Clerk. He'd been working in Hagerstown for almost fifteen years when their grandmother died, and he'd wanted her house *badly*. At the time, Bonnie was still fairly new to the area herself, so she didn't understand why her partners at the law firm were so intent on settling the estate in his favor. To *her*, Ethan had always come off as pushy and entitled.

But his opinion mattered to Natalie. And he had softened a little...after Nat had split her inheritance with him.

"I don't really know him any better than you do." Natalie sighed at Bonnie's cop-out, so she added, "but either way, the real question is, why do you want so badly for him to like you?"

Nat stared at a spot on the floor, her face blank. Bonnie recognized this as a good sign–Natalie was actually hearing and considering her question now, instead of simply opposing it.

"I don't like the way Mom ended things with Dad," she said slowly. "Ethan and I were never given the option of being siblings. We never had a chance to even try to like each other.

"And you know, maybe if we did we'd still have ended up hating each other. We can't know one way or the other how it would have gone. But... I don't want that decision to have been made *for* us, you know? I want the chance to get to meet him, and his wife, and my future niece or nephew. I want them to get the chance to meet me."

She met Bonnie's gaze then, and there was something new sparkling in her blue-green eyes. Her grandmother's eyes. Bonnie recognized it as that same determination that Sophie had had when she updated her will before she passed.

"You're right. I'm not going to make Ethan like me with roast turkey and pumpkin spice baked alaska. But I can at least get him to meet me halfway, and then we can figure out if we like each other from there."

She gave Bonnie a watery smile, and Bonnie's heart warmed. God, this woman was something else. The way she was just endlessly hopeful, believing in giving people chances and willing to put her heart on the chopping block for a chance at a family connection.

"But where does that leave your mom and her boyfriend?" Bonnie couldn't help playing devil's advocate; there were just so many places Natalie's dinner plans could go awry. Even more than they already had.

Natalie took a deep breath. "Okay, this is going to sound silly, but bear with me, okay?" Bonnie nodded. "Mom could have had Christmas dinner literally anywhere. She works with tons of restaurants, has a whole slew of connections, I mean, she's got a whole life here that has mattered more to her than me since I graduated high school.

"But like, she called *me*, to ask to do Christmas dinner together. She *wanted* to spend it with me. For the first time in over ten years, Bonnie. How could I say no to that?"

Bonnie was quiet as she tried to imagine what she'd do if her parents called her out of the blue after all these years and invited her to Christmas dinner. Even though they'd kicked her out at seventeen, after she'd been expelled from Catholic School for kissing another girl in the library, there was a part of her that craved their approval. Their love.

She knew she'd never get it. But if an invitation to Christmas dinner with the Bakers was on the table, it would still be hard for her to refuse.

Slowly, Bonnie nodded. "Okay. I get it."

"Am I crazy?"

"Yes." She smiled. "But I knew that already."

"Do you still want me to cancel?"

Natalie was looking at her with a mix of guilt and anxiety in her eyes. Bonnie sighed.

The truth was, she still didn't think it was the best plan. But she at least had a slightly better understanding of why it was so important to her. And she was still determined to see Operation Supportive Girlfriend through.

"No, you don't have to cancel. *But!*" Bonnie shouted over the smile that prematurely stretched from ear-to-ear. "You have to ask Ethan and Clara and Michelle to bring a dish. I'm not handling all of the sides by myself. I'm sure they won't be *that* upset about it. Tell them you sprained your wrist and ankle. They'll understand."

"Deal," Natalie said, giving her a soft smile. "I'm sorry that I'm putting you through this, honey. I know it isn't your thing." She squeezed Bonnie's fingers. Bonnie squeezed back.

"It's okay. We'll get through it." Bonnie laughed. "And who knows? Maybe by the end of all of this, I'll know how to cook!"

Natalie scrunched her face. "Now that *would* be a Christmas miracle!"

Bonnie rolled her eyes, and got up to refill their coffee. While Natalie was turned away from her in her chair, finishing her bagel, Bonnie lingered for an extra moment at the coffee pot.

As much as she hated it, she knew it was time to call in reinforcements. She snuck her phone out of her pocket and texted Shawn.

ME

I think Natalie and I might need your assistance. Are you free today to help our girl get the turkey ready?

CHAPTER 12

*A*fter they finished breakfast and talked through a plan for that evening and the next morning, Bonnie headed to work. Natalie called Clara and her mom to ask them if they could each bring a dish since she wasn't able to make all of them after all, and they, surprisingly, agreed. Then she sat herself down to see if she could pare down the menu for the next day. With Clara and Michelle contributing, did she and Bonnie really need to make six side dishes? Or would four suffice? She pondered as her pencil hovered over the list, poised to cross out the cranberry ambrosia salad she'd planned on setting in the fridge overnight.

She really wasn't up for being on her feet—*foot*— for an hour to get all the ingredients together for it. Maybe they could settle for just the canned cranberry sauce this year.

No sooner had she scribbled that and the lemon-glazed saffron buns off her list did the doorbell ring. She tried to pry herself out of her chair and her ankle gave a twinge.

"Coming!" She hollered at the door, hunting for her crutch, when she heard it swing open on its own. "What the–"

"I let myself in, I hope you're not naked!" Shawn poked his

BETTING ON THE BIRD

head in through the crack in the door with his hand over his eyes. "Unless you're cool with that, in which case—"

"Shawn! What the hell are you doing here?" Natalie's tone was good-humored as she slumped back into the chair, grateful she didn't have to get up. *I am so glad he's got an extra key.*

"So from your late-night text, I'm guessing you found the Elf on the Shelf?" He peeked through his fingers, a wide, shit-eating grin taking up the lower half of his face.

The smile she'd been wearing instantly morphed into a glare. "Yes. And I have the bruise on my ass to prove it."

"Did it scare you that bad?" As Shawn made his way into the house, Natalie realized he was dragging what looked like a model spaceship behind him. She craned her neck so she could get a better view down the hallway from the kitchen.

"Shawn, what is—"

"Bonnie texted and said you needed reinforcements!" He grunted, planting the metal contraption in front of the kitchen table and spreading his hands in a "Ta-da!" Gesture.

She blinked. "From space?"

"No, silly, for the turkey! Ain't you never seen a turkey fryer before?"

"Oh no." Natalie put her hands up. "No way, Shawn. I've ordered a perfectly beautiful organic heritage turkey which should be in the mail today, and I'm not going to ruin it by drowning it in oil. I've got enough on my plate—"

"Nat, Nat, Nat. *You're* not going to be frying anything. I am!" Shawn put his hands on his hips like a superhero and gave her a toothy grin. "I feel awful about falling on top of you the other night. And I know you had this big ol' feast planned for your mom and brother, and you shouldn't be liftin' a heavy roasting pan with your wrist all messed up. Then I found this guy in one of my grandpa's kitchen cabinets and I thought it was the perfect solution to your problem!" He put his hand on top of the giant metal contraption, lifted its lid, and pulled out a package from inside. "I even got this to wear while I handle the bird!"

Natalie stared, slack-jawed, as Shawn unfolded a wad of red fabric, revealing a Santa hat and an apron with a picture of a turkey and the words **Ready to Get Basted and Stuffed** on it.

She blushed. "Shawn! You can't wear that in front of my mother!"

He eyed her up and down. "Is she single? Cause if she's as pretty as you–" She leaned forward to smack him, but he jumped out of the way. "I'm just kiddin'. I brought this one, too, just in case."

He revealed another lump of fabric from somewhere, and unfolded it to reveal a green apron emblazoned with the phrase **Single and Ready to Jingle**.

She shook her head. "Shawn..."

He ignored her, piling up the aprons on the table and grabbing the deep fryer. "Where can I put this baby? On the deck? Probably the safest place for it."

Recognizing that he was a man on a mission, she let him carry the giant appliance out the sliding glass door to the back porch. Unlike the porch in front of the house, this one of the areas they'd yet to spruce up in all of their home improvement projects: the deck boards were splintered and uneven, and as she watched Shawn struggle to find a level spot to perch the fryer, her unease grew.

"You sure that it would be safe to fry a turkey out here?" She limped over to the open door and peeked through. The cold air felt simultaneously good on her aching wrist and biting on her fingers. She rubbed her upper arm with her good hand. "It's not exactly the most sturdy location..."

"Ah, it's fine, Nat! You worry too much. I was on this roof once..."

She grabbed a sweater from the back of a kitchen chair and

joined Shawn outside while he told horror stories from the various dangerous odd jobs he'd taken over the years. Patching roofs that were about to cave in, fighting a family of squirrels that had moved into the gutters he'd been hired to clean, slipping on a floor joist and falling right onto a 2x12 between his legs.

"The doc said if I hadn'ta caught myself, I'd likely be sterile!" Natalie winced, and Shawn winked at her. "Luckily, I just broke my wrist instead."

"You're unbelievable..."

"And *you're* all set up to fry a turkey this year! Now all we need's the bird. Where is it? I wanna make sure it fits."

"It should be arriving today in the mail." Natalie whipped out her phone to double-check the confirmation email.

"Wait—like, a frozen turkey?" Shawn's face fell. "You know you gotta thaw those, right?"

"I was just gonna run it under water in the sink. How long can it take, an hour?" She found the confirmation, and held out her phone to him. "Yep. On the way, expected delivery by 8pm today."

Shawn scanned the tiny screen. "Nat, it's an eighteen-pound turkey. It's gonna take way longer to thaw than an hour. Mom's been thawing ours in the fridge for days."

"*Days??*" She snatched her phone back. "No way. Are you serious?" She brought up Google. Sure enough, recommendations for anywhere from 24-96 hours to thaw a turkey greeted her.

She groaned. "I didn't even *think* about thawing the damn thing! Shit!" She sank onto one of the wooden steps and winced when the wood creaked. She hung her head in her hands. "Maybe I should just buy a ham or something instead."

"Ham?" Shawn plopped down beside her, causing the stair to cry out further objections. "But you ordered that special. And I brought over the deep fryer!"

She snorted, but he continued. "Nat, you got me and your girlfriend to help you out. It's gonna be fine."

"No it's not," Natalie sniffled. Oh jeez, was she *crying*? She wiped her nose on her sleeve and it came away soaked. Yep. She was crying. "The Kitchenaid's broken, the turkey's frozen, and my baked alaska keeps melting!"

"What's baked alaska?"

"It's like this fancy dessert cake with ice cream and meringue on it. It's supposed to be delicious, but the ice cream keeps melting in the oven."

"Why are you putting the ice cream in the oven?"

Natalie wiped her eyes again. "The meringue is supposed to insulate it. Keep it from melting."

Shawn frowned. "I don't know much about baking, but I know you ain't supposed to make ice cream in the oven. Can't you insulate it with something else?"

"Like what? Frozen peas?" She snorted. "Anything I could would still melt."

"Hmm." Just then, the doorbell rang. Natalie went to go see who it was, but Shawn put a hand on her shoulder. "I got it. You stay here."

Natalie sniffed some more out in the cold, eyes glazing as she took in the bare branches of the trees all around her yard. The detached garage looked worn-down on the edge of her property, and she wondered once again how she was going to deliver Shawn the vintage car that was still parked in there. Now that he was helping her out with dinner, she really needed to make sure she got him his gift. So many grand plans she'd had for Christmas, and they were all falling apart before her eyes.

"Hey Nat! It's the turkey!" Shawn called out from the kitchen. "Come in here!"

Reluctantly, she got back up and made her way to the

kitchen, and was greeted by Shawn's relentless grin once again. He held out his hands.

"So I've got good news and bad news," he began. "The bad news is, the turkey is frozen solid because they packed it in dry ice. But the good news is, I think I have an idea how to keep your baked Nevada from melting."

CHAPTER 13

"Wear these. Otherwise you might burn yourself."

The day had arrived. Bonnie, Natalie, and Shawn were all gathered in Natalie's kitchen, after all three of them had stayed up late the night before to assemble side dishes. Natalie had directed, Shawn had chopped and prepped, and Bonnie had mixed and assembled.

They had a schedule written out for the oven, calculated down to the minute, to make sure they had enough time to get all of Christmas Dinner baked in time.

And now, Shawn was handing Bonnie a pair of leather gloves so she could cover the pumpkin spice ice cream dome in a layer of dry ice pellets.

"Are you sure this is the way we should be doing this?" Bonnie eyed the gloves warily. "Is this sound? Did we Google it?"

"What's there to Google? Dry ice keeps things cold, and your ice cream keeps melting. This'll make a cold layer between the egg stuff and the ice cream so it won't turn to soup!"

"Meringue, Shawn. It's called meringue."

Natalie was in pure panic mode, and she already sounded

exhausted. For the second night in a row, she hadn't been able to sleep. Bonnie knew this, because her constant tossing and turning had kept her awake most of the night as well.

She was in the middle of quadruple-checking the schedule, her phone calculator up as she checked her math on the timing for the 30th time. Blue-tinged circles lined the skin under her eyes, and her hair was a nest of staticky flyaways from the number of times she'd run her fingers through it. The sleeves of her obnoxious Christmas sweater were pushed up past her elbows, as the kitchen was a toasty seventy-six degrees with the oven and toaster oven going. Not to mention the heaters, which they'd turned up last night to make up for the sudden cold front that swooped in in the middle of the night.

Shawn shoved the gloves into Bonnie's hands and waved away the woman's fears. "Just trust me on this, Bonnie. I'm gonna check on the turkey."

He slid out the door to the back deck, where he'd rigged up a cooler with a water pump to circulate water around the heritage turkey to thaw it faster. She had to admit, it was an impressive solution, and it did demonstrate that he was a man to be trusted. She'd been right to ask him for help the day before.

And yet, Bonnie was still a little tense around Shawn. She'd wished she could have been there for Natalie yesterday, could have been the one to actually convince her that things were going to be okay. But she'd had to go to work, which had cut their conversation short. Bonnie cursed her case-load, which had of course doubled leading up to the holidays, and yesterday had been her last day in the office for the year. The Law Office of Sheffield, Yang, and Baker was closed for the week between Christmas and New Year's, which meant that they all had to scramble to finish their last piles of paperwork.

So she'd had no choice but to call in backup, and for Natalie, the best backup was Shawn.

By the time she'd gotten to the house after work on Friday,

the two of them had already prepped all the veggies and planned out the entire day without her, and Natalie seemed to be leaning on him way more than she had Bonnie over the past week.

Bonnie knew she wasn't the best cook or baker (ironically, considering her last name). While her female classmates in law school had stress-baked their way through studying for the LSATs, she had been more of the stress-hookup type.

Nat, however, was not the type to reach for comfort in the same way. She withdrew into herself when she was overwhelmed, and Bonnie didn't know how to deal with that. Other than their quickie on Monday morning and Bonnie's consolation of Natalie that Wednesday night, they'd hardly gotten any time to themselves that week. And it felt like when they weren't having sex, they were fighting. It wouldn't bother her so much if Natalie was closed off to everyone else in the same way, but she wasn't. She'd spent plenty of time with Shawn while Bonnie had been at work, and they were still getting along fine. She'd let him in, and accepted his help.

Which made Bonnie feel like an outsider in her own relationship.

She sighed, looking at the smoking bowl of dry ice pellets that Shawn had picked up that morning to save their baked alaska. Then she donned the gloves, unwrapped the ice cream and proceeded to pat a thick layer of pellets around the frozen dome.

"Make sure you cover the bottom, too." Natalie didn't even look up from her schedule when she corrected her.

"Yep," Bonnie answered through grit teeth. *Just one more day...*

Once this dinner was over, Natalie wouldn't have to worry about it anymore and they could actually relax together for the remainder of the holiday. They could watch cheesy movies, order Chinese food, and Bonnie would have a whole glorious week where she wouldn't have to go into the office. If they wanted, they could even stay in bed the whole time.

The thought of having Natalie's relaxed, naked body all to herself on Christmas Day kept Bonnie's determination alive as she placed the now dry ice-coated ice cream dome back into the bowl of pellets to wait for piping. She then looked to Natalie for further instructions.

"What's next, Nat?"

"Umm... one sec." Natalie was distracted by her phone buzzing with a call. "Hi Clara! You and Ethan still good for 4:00?"

She paused while she listened to the other end of the call, and then winced. "Umm..." she consulted her schedule. "Suuure, that should work..."

She made a few scribbles on the graph paper and nodded along to the conversation. "Understandable. Mothers, right? We love 'em!"

While Bonnie could tell she was trying to be funny, the frustration in her voice was evident. The result made her sound slightly hysterical.

"Uh-huh. Yep. Okay, we'll see you at three then!" As soon as she hung up the phone, she flung herself down onto the table. Her forehead hit the wood with a loud *thunk*, and Bonnie heard a muffled "Ow."

"Honey? What's wrong?"

"Ethan's mother needs to use their oven for some triple-baked something-or-other family Christmas loaf thing, so Clara asked if she could warm up their casserole in *our* oven instead. *'It'll only take an hour!'*"

She said that last bit in a high-pitched voice, imitating Clara. Bonnie's heart sunk.

"And... you said she could, I take it?"

"Well, I couldn't tell her no! She's in charge of the sweet potato casserole! Remember? You had told me to ask the others to bring a dish?" She looked at Bonnie as if surprised she even had to clarify. "Besides, she sounded tired. Apparently the baby kept moving and kicking all night."

It was all she could do not to snap back at her. She'd told her to ask the others to bring a dish to lower her stress, not give her more to worry about. And now Natalie was making it sound like it was making things more difficult for her.

"Are you seriously angry at me for that?"

"No–not angry, just frustrated with everything, okay? You're fine. Everything is fine."

"What do you need me to do?" Her voice had gotten louder without her realizing it. They were practically shouting now.

"Just give me a second, okay?" Natalie jabbed her finger at her phone to get back to her calculator and proceeded to ignore her for the next thirty seconds.

But it felt like much longer. Bonnie's patience began to wear thin. *This whole thing is ridiculous. While I'm waiting for her to calculate this out, we could be baking already!*

She knew that Natalie's list had been calculated down to the last degree for cooking temperature and accounted for the serving order, but it seemed like she was making it a lot harder than it had to be. Bonnie could help, dammit. She *was* helping!

And she wasn't going to sit around and do nothing while her girlfriend had a panic attack.

The preheat timer went off, and Bonnie made her move. "I'm just going to put in the green beans, okay?"

"No, wait–that's supposed to be after the potato buns."

"I thought we just warmed those up at the end in the toaster oven?"

"Oh–right, not the buns, the scalloped potatoes, I mean. Is the cream sauce ready to go?"

"Yes, Nat, we made it last night, remember? It's in the fridge with the other casseroles–"

"Wait! Did we remember the fried onions?" Natalie's voice

rose in pitch as she heaved herself out of the chair and limped over to the pantry. Bonnie set down the green beans and scrambled to help her. "I don't think I remembered to put them on the list—"

"Honey, stop, you're going to hurt yourself—"

"I'm *fine*, Bonnie, just *give me a second!*" Natalie screeched, pushing Bonnie away. On one leg, she whipped open the pantry door and started rummaging through the shelves noisily. Bonnie threw her hands up in the air, stomped over to the counter, and grabbed the tin of fried onions that she'd set out the night before.

She started back toward the pantry to show her the tin, but before she could, Natalie added, "You forgot them, didn't you? I *knew* I should have done the shopping!"

Bonne froze, appalled, as Natalie continued to scramble through the pantry. She watched her dig to the back of each shelf, muttering to herself, before her disbelief gave way to anger.

"Natalie!" Bonnie snapped, holding out the tin and shaking it. Natalie snapped her head around and her face widened in surprise.

"Oh! We did have some…"

"No, we didn't. I picked them up after work on Monday when I went to the store." Bonnie slammed the tin on the table, making Natalie's grandma's silver candlesticks rattle against each other. "And to clarify, *no*, they *weren't* on the list. But I picked them up anyway because I remembered that we needed them for green bean casserole, which is your favorite part of any holiday dinner! Remember that? When we spent Thanksgiving together, just the two of us?"

Natalie's mouth opened slightly as Bonnie finally erupted. Realization dawned in her eyes, and her face fell.

At least she has the good sense to look sorry. Bonnie's chest heaved as she stepped toward the pantry.

"Remember how great that was, Nat? We just made a little roaster chicken together and some mashed potatoes, and you scoured the penny saver for the one grocery store that had cream of mushroom soup on sale because you refused to pay $2.50 per can? I thought it was so cute how particular you were about it, and how insistent you were that it be perfect because it was our first big holiday together. And you know what? It was perfect. It was small, and sweet, and low stress, and everything was delicious.

"But now? Honey, your perfectionism is ruining this whole day! You had to get the most expensive, top-of-the-line turkey to impress Ethan, and it's still frozen. You have to make the most intricate dessert of all time to please your mother and her chef boyfriend, so you've got me coating *ice cream* in *dry ice* so it doesn't *melt in the oven!* You're bending over backwards to accommodate everyone when you've already spent an entire week planning to the last detail, when you could have just called it off or pushed it back an hour and nobody would have cared!

"And now you want to blame *me* for forgetting something that *you* didn't put on the list, when I fucking *did it anyway*? When I've been spending every day helping you get everything ready? What the actual *fuck*, Nat? Can't you see I'm trying to help you here?? Why won't you just *let me*? You're so obsessed with throwing the perfect Christmas and impressing everyone else that you can't even see that *I* already love you just the way you are!"

Bonnie dragged in a huge, shaking breath, and wiped her eyes. Tears had blurred her vision as she talked, but she hadn't cared. She couldn't believe how useless Natalie assumed she was. How she felt she couldn't trust her.

"Why couldn't we just have this be a quiet Christmas, too? With just the two of us again? Instead of this... this..." Bonnie's shoulders shook with sobs, and they swallowed the rest of whatever she was going to say.

She understood that Natalie wanted a family Christmas. And there was nothing wrong with that. But Natalie *was* Bonnie's family now. She was all Bonnie had, and all she'd wanted was for them to have a night together to decorate their tree and watch Hallmark movies. Before they had to come out to her brother. Before she had to prove herself to another parent who would only reject her.

"Bonnie..." Natalie began, but faltered when Bonnie turned from her to grab a tissue to blow her nose.

She was a mess. A gross, snotty, crying mess, and she was ruining Natalie's Christmas dinner anyway, even after trying so hard to help make it happen.

"Now *I* need a minute, okay? Just...have Shawn put the first casserole in."

She grabbed the box of tissues and walked out of the kitchen.

CHAPTER 14

God, I am a total bitch.

Natalie stood helplessly in the open pantry, still staring unblinkingly at the patio door through which Bonnie had stormed outside. *How did I even let this happen?*

For a moment, despite the fact that time was something she didn't have to spare, she thought back to the quiet Thanksgiving she and Bonnie had had just a few weeks ago. She roasted a 6-pound chicken, Bonnie had whipped up some instant mashed potatoes, and yes, Natalie had in fact scoured the little local paper for the neighborhood grocer's deal on cream of mushroom soup and fried onions so she could make her favorite green bean casserole.

Bonnie had picked up a bottle of regional Virginia wine for them to split and toast their first holiday together. Then they'd watched the *Kill Bill* movies and spent the night arguing over who was hornier for Uma Thurman, before snuggling up by the fireplace and eventually falling asleep.

It was actually the success of their little Thanksgiving dinner that made her want to recreate that kind of magic with her family. She thought if she and Bonnie could create such a perfect Thanksgiving dinner with just the two of them, surely they could put on a great Christmas celebration, too. And maybe it would be enough to make her and her brother feel like actual family.

Shawn slid open the door to the back porch and peeked his head in. "Everything okay in here?"

Natalie sniffed. "No. I'm the worst."

"What makes you say that?" Shawn stepped inside, wiped his boots on the mat and walked over to her. "Did you forget something?"

He looked over her plans scattered out across the table. As she'd brainstormed, plotted, and planned out the perfect family Christmas dinner over the past weeks, she'd completely lost sight of the things that had made Thanksgiving so wonderful in the first place. Natalie's vision blurred as tears filled her eyes.

"Yeah. My girlfriend."

Shawn looked confused. "She just went outside–"

"I know where she went, Shawn!" Natalie snapped, causing him to jump back and throw his hands up in front of his face. Her eyes widened in horror as she realized what she'd just done. Again. "Oh my God, Shawn, I'm so sorry. *Fuck!* What is wrong with me?"

She slumped against the pantry door, her ankle throbbing as she'd been resting her weight on it for far longer than she should have. Another sob wracked her shoulders and she rubbed more tears from her eyes. "I'm a fucking Christmas tyrant. This dinner, this whole thing–it's taken over my life!"

Shawn's eyebrows furrowed in concern as he slowly approached her. She let him help her into one of the kitchen chairs, then he sat across from her, steeping his fingers on the table.

"It's your first family Christmas dinner. That's a big deal,"

Shawn said sympathetically. "You should see my mom on Thanksgiving every year. Mel and I call it "Operation Dessert Storm." He chuckled at his own joke.

Natalie snorted. "Does she blow up at you and your sister for forgetting ingredients when you've been helping her the entire week before, too?"

Shawn squinted. "No way. She doesn't trust us to do any of the shopping."

Natalie winced, remembering her exclamation. *I knew I should have done the shopping...*

Except she was wrong. She hadn't even remembered the thing she'd been searching for. Bonnie had. She'd remembered, and all because she loved Natalie, and knew her well enough to know she'd want fired onions on her green bean casserole for Christmas dinner. Meanwhile, Natalie had been so caught up in her own stress over the whole event that she hadn't even noticed how much Bonnie had been keeping everything together.

She looked up at Shawn, who was smiling his goofy grin at her. He'd been helping her too, after Bonnie had called and asked him for help. And she hadn't even said thank you.

"I don't know why she wouldn't. You've been an absolute lifesaver to *me* this weekend." Natalie sighed, glancing over at her plans.

"And to think, this is the first family dinner I've ever helped cook!"

Natalie smiled at him and shook her head. The people that were here at the house right now? They *were* Natalie's family. At least, her chosen family. It made sense that the three of them were working together to make this dinner happen.

As she consulted the plans strewn across the table, she realized Bonnie had been right. The green bean casserole *was* supposed to go into the oven first.

"Can you put the green beans in the oven for me?" She asked, setting a timer on her phone and grabbing her crutch. "I need to go find Bonnie and make this right."

"Sure thing," Shawn said. He nodded towards the back door. "I think she's handling the turkey."

CHAPTER 15

  *B*onnie was not handling the turkey. In fact, she was nowhere near the deep fryer or the back porch. Natalie eventually found her in the chilly garage, perched on the hood of her grandfather's old Chevy Bel Air with a tall boy of PBR in her hand, staring off into the distance.

She took a deep breath as she peeked in through the side window. *Here goes nothing.*

"Hey, honey," Natalie hedged, hobbling in through the side door.

Bonnie waved without looking at her. Instead, her eyes stared unseeing at an oil stain on the cracked concrete floor. "Don't you have gourmet gravy to whisk to impress your mom?"

Natalie winced. Okay. She deserved that.

"No. Shawn's handling things for a minute. I have something more important I need to do."

Bonnie looked up then, hurt still evident in her red-rimmed eyes. Even behind her glasses, Natalie could see that she'd been crying. Something she hadn't actually seen Bonnie ever do before.

Her unflappable girlfriend, the lawyer. Driven to tears by *her* perfectionism.

"Bonnie, I'm so sorry."

She didn't move. Just kept staring at Natalie as if waiting for her to continue. So, she grabbed a can of PBR from the open case by the door and rolled her way into a seated position on the hood of the car. It wasn't graceful. And Bonnie didn't make an effort to help.

Finally, she caught her breath, shimmying her butt beneath her and leaning the crutch against the side mirror. She grabbed the beer she'd balanced on the roof of the car and cracked it open, took a sip, and let out another breath to prepare herself for her biggest apology ever.

Bonnie was looking at her expectantly.

"I've got, like, reasons, for why I've been so crazy, but they don't really matter, do they?" Natalie turned her head to meet her girlfriend's eyes, but found very little sympathy there. She wasn't sure what she was supposed to say, other than, "I mean, you know how much I want this dinner to be perfect and all, but I still hurt you. Because I was being awful. I thought I was just like, preventing a bad time at the dinner by thinking everything through and making sure it was perfect, but even if everything I did *did* make the perfect dinner tonight, it still wouldn't be perfect, because you'd still be mad at me."

At that, Bonnie scrunched her nose. "I'm sorry, are you saying this is actually my fault?"

"No!" Natalie shook her head, mortified, "No, of course not! Nothing this whole week has been your fault. You've been amazing. More than amazing. Bonnie, I would have never been able to do any of this without you."

Bonnie's face softened at that. Her shoulders relaxed, and she toyed with the tab on her beer. "Thank you. I have been trying."

Maybe it was the tone of her voice when she said that: small and tired, yet relieved, as if she'd somehow been assuming that Natalie *didn't* appreciate her this whole time, but it broke something in Natalie's chest. Her breath hitched, and tears sprung to her eyes.

"Honey, all of this–" she gestured jerkily with her arms to insinuate the enormity of the Christmas dinner– "it's all because I wanted to bring my family together." She grabbed Bonnie's hand and shook it. "*This?* This is the kind of love I want to feel, but with everyone I abandoned when I moved to L.A."

Bonnie squeezed her fingers, but tilted her head. "What do you mean?"

"You brought up Thanksgiving." Natalie turned towards her a bit, so she could better explain. "How great it was. And it was, wasn't it? It was like, perfect. It made me remember how great family Christmas and Thanksgiving used to be, when I was a little kid. When we had the whole family together, and I didn't have to worry about making sure mom didn't get too stressed, or whether or not Dad was going to pick me up on time for custody. It was just easy and nice and we all wanted to be there. And I thought, with you, with us, being at the center of Christmas this year, maybe I could finally make the family thing work again."

Bonnie studied her for a moment, then looked down at their hands, still intertwined. "But you *are* still worrying about your mom. And your brother. And this time, *you're* the one who's stressed: freaking out about timing, and who's bringing what, and maintaining the peace. Nat, nothing about any of this has been easy or nice." She winced. "I mean, not "nice," you're clearly trying to make it nice, but like, not the way our Thanksgiving was nice. That was nice *because* it was easy. Because we didn't have to impress each other. You're still trying to impress your family."

Natalie blinked. Was that what she was doing? Trying to impress everybody?

She thought about it for a second, letting Bonnie's words sink in. She'd thought she was just trying to bring everyone together. But once her mom had gotten involved, she had started to go a little crazy. "Why is it so much harder with them, Bons?"

Bonnie sighed, and unlatched their hands. She took a sip of her beer before answering. "Because family is just hard, hon. We want it to be easy. We want people to love us just because they're supposed to, but that isn't how it works."

The tears that had been clinging to her eyelashes fell more freely now. Natalie sniffed, and wondered why Bonnie's words were making her so sad. She didn't want to accept that she couldn't have a loving family. She knew she could fix it.

Couldn't she?

Bonnie raised her beer to her lips, then paused. "Or at least, they don't love us because we wow them with a perfect Christmas dinner. They won't love us unless *they* want to."

Natalie considered that for a moment. The two women sat in silence, sipping from their cans, when Shawn burst in through the side door.

"Hey, Nat? Sorry to interrupt…"

She jumped, and slid off the roof of the car, only to wince when her weight sunk onto her bad ankle. She reached for her crutch. "Ahhh–no worries, what's up Shawn?"

"Well, the turkey's just about thawed and I'm gonna need a hand with all the stuff…"

Bonnie appeared at Natalie's side, putting an arm under her shoulder to help take some of the weight off her bad leg. She leaned gratefully into her, taking the gesture as a sign that things between them were at least patched for now. She knew they'd have to talk more later, though. She nodded at Shawn. "Absolutely. I'll–we'll be right there."

He nodded awkwardly before stepping back towards the deck, leaving the garage door open for them.

"I'm still gonna need your help to get this done," Natalie murmured into Bonnie's neck. "If I promise to be better, are you still up for it?"

Bonnie hoisted her up so she could plant a quick kiss on her lips, then she downed the last half of her beer in one, long gulp. "I'll need a few more of these, but sure."

CHAPTER 16

Once they were back in the kitchen and they'd switched the green beans out for the scalloped potatoes, Bonnie laid down a few ground rules.

First, she was opening a bottle of wine.

Second, Natalie was to let her handle putting things in and out of the oven, *without* critique.

And third, she was throwing away the schedule. They had five dishes, four guests on the way, and two hours before the first ones showed up. Dinner would happen, regardless if it was a few minutes late. Natalie could deal with that.

She agreed, on one condition: "I also get to have a glass of wine."

That was a concession Bonnie was only too happy to make.

Two hours later, three casseroles were done, the fourth was in the oven, Bonnie was whipping the meringue for the baked alaska, and Shawn was outside manning the turkey like a seasoned pro. Through the back door, Natalie was able to see him adjusting his quick-thaw cooler setup and preparing the deep fryer with what looked like an entire drum of vegetable oil. She bit her lip at the idea of all of that fat simmering on her back deck. *Is that really as safe as Shawn insists it is?*

She shook her head and took a sip of her wine. She needed to trust the people who were helping her. Bonnie was right: Natalie couldn't control who loved her or why. But here were two people who, for whatever reason, *did* love her, and were proving it. She would be an absolute idiot not to graciously accept their help in making this dinner happen.

Look at me. Learning to be a better person. She smiled over the rim of her wine glass and Bonnie caught it. She smirked at her.

"What are you all smiley about?"

Natalie quickly schooled her features. "Nothing. Just happy."

"Now that you're not freaking out?" Bonnie raised her eyebrows in a knowing look. Nat rolled her eyes.

"Fine, yes, you were right. I needed to chill. Happy?"

"A little, yeah." Bonnie set down the bowl of whipped egg whites and sprinkled the fried onions over the cooling green beans to go back with the other casserole. Then she checked off a line of the list that Natalie had made that morning—the one planning document she hadn't thrown away. "Although I'll be even happier when all of this is over. I love you, honey, but I am so ready to just have an easy, relaxed Christmas with us, some movies, the tree, and a bunch of reheated leftovers."

"That sounds perfect." Natalie grinned, also looking forward to it. "Although I feel it's worth pointing out that we'll only have leftovers *because* we're going through all of this trouble now."

Bonnie tilted her head. "Fair enough."

"Alright, Nat," the kitchen door rumbled as Shawn slid it open and poked his head inside, "I think we're ready for Operation Gobble Gobble."

"Operation Gobble Gobble?" Bonnie's expression warred between amused and incredulous.

"I was gonna call it Operation Heat the Meat, but I didn't want Natalie to slap me. She's been a little scary today." In response, Bonnie slapped him instead. "Hey! Now I said I was *tryin'* to avoid that!"

"What's the status, Shawn?" Natalie asked, making a conscious choice not to let Shawn's words offend her.

"Oil's to temp and the turkey, as far as I can tell, is all thawed. So now, all's that's left is to insert the bird."

"The part we're afraid of. Right." Bonnie sighed. "So what do we need to do here?"

"Well first we gotta unwrap it, and then..." Shawn checked his phone for the instructions, "Season it. So... what are we using for the turkey seasonings?"

Natalie pointed to the counter. "Bonnie, do you see–?"

"On it!" Bonnie grabbed the cardboard box of salt and the tiny jar of poultry seasonings on the counter and handed them to Shawn. He accepted them blindly, still reading his phone in his other hand.

"Got scissors? I'm supposed to unwrap and take out the neck and the gizzards..."

Bonnie hopped across the kitchen and handed him Natalie's kitchen shears. Once again, she felt guilty for ever doubting her girlfriend's capabilities in the kitchen. She really couldn't have handled any of this without her.

"Good luck!" She said as she handed them over to Shawn. He looked up and winked.

"I got this. You got the rest?"

Bonnie held up her bowl of meringue and shot him a relieved smile. "Soft peaks! My wrist is killing me, but I think the hard part is over."

He jostled the spices and scissors and offered a fist for Bonnie to bump. Natalie grinned to herself as she saw her dignified girlfriend return it reluctantly.

This is my real family, she thought. *Right here. Whatever happens, I'm glad I've at least got these two by my side.* Then, the doorbell rang.

"I got it!" Natalie called. Shawn slipped out the back door and Bonnie returned to scooping her meringue into a piping bag. She grabbed her crutch and slowly made her way to the front door, where Ethan and Clara were waiting.

"Merry Christmas!"

Natalie blinked in surprise as she took in the full stomach of her sister-in-law, who looked about ready to pop. *She really is due any day, isn't she?* A brief stab of guilt knotted in her stomach until Ethan's head poked out from behind his wife's frame, and he supported her up the small step into the foyer.

"Merry Christmas, you guys. Thank you so much for coming."

"Thank you for hosting," Ethan said. Once Clara was inside, he handed over a tall, skinny gift bag that looked like it held a bottle of wine. "For tonight. It's a white."

"Amazing! I'll set it on ice!" Natalie led the way into the kitchen, the gift bag bouncing lightly against her leg as she hobbled forward. They were a fairly slow caravan, with Clara waddling behind her, and Ethan stepping purposefully with his hands up in an attempt to prevent any accidents in the ten feet between the foyer and the dining room.

Bonnie's back was turned to them as they made their way to the table and Clara set down her casserole dish. She made a face, letting out a breath and rubbing her stomach. Ethan pulled out a chair for her. Natalie watched as she settled in gingerly and the two of them looked at each other with a gaze that held multitudes.

Seeing the way they cared for each other tugged at Nat's heart. The concern her brother had for his wife and their unborn child was nothing short of touching. She almost felt bad witnessing their exchange, as if she'd stumbled onto a private moment.

She gave them a minute, turning instead to her own partner, who was absorbed in her task at the counter. The warmth filling her chest spread all the way to her toes. Clara wasn't the only lucky woman in this kitchen; Natalie also had someone who would go to incredible lengths for her.

By the time Ethan had gotten Clara settled and lowered himself into his own chair, Bonnie had just finished piping the meringue onto the frozen dome.

"Alright! Now we'll just pop that into the oven when we finish up the green beans," she announced. Then she spotted Ethan and Clara.

Natalie watched as her girlfriend took a deep breath, and held out her hand. "Ethan. So nice to see you outside of the office. Merry Christmas."

A look of confusion passed her brother's face for a moment, as if he was trying to place where he'd last seen Bonnie. It only took a second for recognition to light his eyes, and he hesitantly grasped her hand. "Ms. Baker?"

"Yes, Ethan, Clara," Natalie gestured between the three of them. "You've met Bonnie. Or as I like to call her, my girlfriend."

Bonnie flinched at her clumsy introduction. She swallowed. She really should have thought that through a little more.

"We started dating after the dust settled on the estate," Bonnie clarified. It was a half-truth. Natalie and Bonnie hadn't realized who each other were until after the first time they'd slept together, and it wasn't until a month after that, when Natalie officially decided to stay in Maryland, that they'd decided to give their relationship a chance. But that had been such a chaotic time in Nat's life that she couldn't really separate any of it in her mind. She'd been drawn to Bonnie from the moment she'd met her. And now that she was here, she really couldn't picture her life in Maryland without her.

Regardless, here they were. And she was determined to make the most of it.

"It's so nice to see you again, Bonnie," Clara said brightly, elbowing Ethan in the ribs as he looked wide-eyed between the two women. "It looks like you and Natalie have been working hard!"

"Bonnie's been amazing. She's practically put this whole thing together since I sprained my ankle." Natalie gestured with her crutch, and shot Bonnie a grateful look.

She smiled back at her, and Clara and Ethan shared another look. "It's so nice to see you making a home here, Natalie," Clara said.

Then all three women turned to Ethan, as if waiting for his acceptance of the situation. He cleared his throat, and nodded, before tilting his head to his sister. "Yes. It's nice to see what you've done with the place. It looks like you're settling in well."

Natalie let out a breath. "I'm excited to make a lot of good memories here."

The four of them settled into a contemplative and slightly awkward silence for a moment, and Natalie fought the nervousness that tugged at her stomach. The weight of this dinner, and her desire to rekindle some kind of family tradition with the holidays, paralyzed her in the quiet kitchen, and she scrambled to figure out something to say. Luckily, Bonnie was able to break the ice.

"So Clara, how long does your casserole need to be in the oven?"

"Oh! Only half an hour or so. I baked it last night, we just need to warm it up."

"Perfect! I'll set the temp." Bonnie grabbed the dish off the table, and Natalie made her way to the cabinets.

"Can I get everyone something to drink?" She leaned her crutch against the counter and balanced on her good foot as she pulled out some glasses for the guests.

"I'll have a glass of wine," Ethan settled into a chair at the table. "Clara?"

"Water is fine for me," she said, settling her hands on her stomach. Natalie poured a glass from the bottle she and Bonnie had already opened for Ethan, and navigated the kitchen to get everyone some water from the filter in the fridge.

CRASH.

"What the–" Bonnie whipped around from her crouch by the oven, where she'd just put the two casseroles.

Natalie's first instinct had been to turn to the stove, but she quickly turned to the back door once she realized the source of the noise.

Shawn wrenched open the door, face white with panic. "Do y'all have a fire extinguisher?"

"What happened?" Ethan burst up from the table, eyes wide.

"Uhh–" Shawn began, before Natalie screamed, pointing to the back deck.

"FIRE!"

The five of them froze in terror as flames flickered to life across the dry, splintering wooden boards of her back deck. Bonnie sprung into action in the kitchen, flinging open cabinet doors to find a fire extinguisher. Ethan shouted to Natalie.

"Quick! Do you have any blankets?"

"Umm–the living room! There's an afghan on the couch!"

"Here!" Bonnie shouted, shoving a red cylinder into Shawn's hands. "Put it out!"

Natalie hadn't even known there *was* a fire extinguisher in the cabinets. She wondered for a second how long it had been hiding under her sink.

Meanwhile, Clara pulled her phone from her purse and dialed 911. Ethan and Natalie hunted for blankets and towels. She grabbed a stack from the laundry room and darted out the door.

The sight that greeted her was pure chaos. Shawn was struggling with the pin of the old extinguisher while stomping on small bursts of self-contained fire that looked as if they had been sprinkled all across her back yard. The fryer was consumed in a giant plume of flame, Which Ethan tried (in vain) to smother with a towel. Natalie hauled herself in a loping jog to the side of the house, ignoring the protests of her bad leg, where she remembered seeing the turkey thaw in a cooler full of water. She spotted it, grabbed the vessel, and ignored her protesting leg as she dragged its heavy weight behind her and hurried to the deck.

Shawn tossed the old extinguisher aside just in time to see Natalie with the cooler. "Nat! No!"

But it was too late. She bent over and used her good arm to fling the plastic cooler full of water across the back yard, where the icy liquid splashed across the deck. But instead of putting out the flames, the wave of droplets crashed and sizzled and spit wherever they made contact with the fire, spreading out the miniature flames and sending the deck into further chaos.

"Jesus Christ!" Ethan shouted, jumping back from the hopping flames and patting at his sleeves, which were now smoking, "It's a grease fire, Natalie!"

"Fuck! I'm so sorry!" She twisted away from the heat and shifted painfully onto her ankle, before sinking to the ground. "Ah—!"

"Quick! Get to the front yard!"

Bonnie's voice echoed against the side of the garage as sirens sounded in the distance. Natalie half-limped, half-crawled to the driveway and away from the flames. Her heart pounded, and she cursed herself for being so stupid as to pour water on a grease fire. What had she been thinking?

She felt an arm reach around her, and looked up to see Bonnie supporting her. She helped her to the front yard, while Shawn helped Clara, who had her phone against her ear. Ethan ran through the house to join them, still patting at his sleeves. He descended on Clara and Shawn, immediately checking to see if his wife was unharmed.

Natalie gave Bonnie a panicked look, and the two women rushed over as fast as they could. Shawn ran to their side, helping with Natalie's weight so they could stay upright. Tears sprung to Nat's eyes as the three of them held each other, and the five of them waited for what felt like an eternity as smoke began to billow from out behind the house.

"Oh God, the casserole!" Bonnie groaned, and went to head back into the kitchen. Natalie grabbed her shirt.

"What are you thinking?? Fuck the casserole!" Nat yelled. Around them, the sirens got louder and louder. "Let the pros handle it!"

"But—the green beans–"

"Bonnie," Clara said calmly. "We really don't need to worry about the green beans right now."

The five of them stared at the house for a moment, until Shawn snorted. Then Ethan's shoulders began to shake, and pretty soon Bonnie, Natalie, and Clara were all laughing uncontrollably in a tired heap on the front lawn. Bonnie wheezed out a reply.

"You're right, you're right—if I'd have grabbed anything, it probably should have been the wine!"

The five of them laughed even harder, especially Natalie, who could have sworn something inside her had finally snapped.

"Stop–stop, my bladder isn't what it used to be–" Clara started to say, then gasped and clutched her stomach. "Oof!"

"Honey? Are you okay?" Ethan's tone switched from jovial to concerned as he wrapped an arm around his wife.

"Fine, fine, just an–oh!" Her face scrunched and she bent over further, and Ethan turned white as a sheet. "Ooooooh, fudge, honey..."

Natalie looked from Clara to Ethan, and then to Bonnie. "Oh shit. We might need more than just the fire department."

Luckily, they didn't have to wait long. By the time Clara's first contraction had passed, firefighters, cops, and an ambulance had descended upon the small farmhouse.

CHAPTER 17

The paramedics descended on Clara and were checking her vitals by the ambulance. Bonnie was chatting with one of the firefighters about the oven, while three others took to the backyard to tackle the turkey fryer.

Shawn shuffled his toes, hunched over in his jacket in the middle of the front lawn. Natalie limped over to him, her entire leg now throbbing uncomfortably. She wondered briefly if she'd injured it further when she'd tossed the cooler onto the flames. It was hurting a lot more than it had been earlier in the day.

"I ruined your Christmas party," Shawn mumbled. "I'm sorry, Nat."

Natalie shook her head, leaning against his tall body to take the weight off her ankle. "You didn't ruin it. It was an accident. It happens."

The two of them looked at the smoke billowing from behind the roof line. She winced. "I just hope the house survives."

"It will." Bonnie walked over and snaked an arm around Natalie's waist. Between the two of them, she was able to balance on only her good foot. "I just finished talking to the fireman. None of the grease got into the house, thank God, although the green bean casserole is ruined. Sorry, hon."

Nat snorted. "It's okay. Can you help me get over to Clara? I want to make sure she's okay."

She and Bonnie shuffled over to the ambulance, where they'd loaded Clara onto a stretcher. Ethan was holding her hand and staring at his phone. As they approached, Clara's face crumpled and she gritted her teeth.

"That's eleven minutes," Ethan announced. "Should I drive her, or should we ride in the ambulance?"

"Let's load her in," the paramedic answered. Then he noticed Natalie. "Miss, are you okay?"

"It's a previous injury." She waved a hand. "Please. Pregnant woman is more important."

Ethan shot her a grateful smile. "Raincheck on dinner?"

"Absolutely. Merry Christmas!"

After waving off a couple more concerned paramedics, Bonnie and Natalie stepped out of the way so the ambulance could pull out of her skinny driveway. Meanwhile, Bonnie eyed her girlfriend up and down.

"Did you hurt yourself more? You're holding your leg up."

"I may have aggravated the fracture a little when I threw the cooler on the fire," Natalie admitted. Bonnie stared at her.

"Why didn't you say something earlier??"

She rolled her eyes. "Bonnie, Clara was going into labor and my house was on fire. I think those take precedence."

"For fuck's sake..." Bonnie hoisted Nat towards her sedan and wrenched open the door.

"What are you doing?" Nat gave a disgruntled "oomph!" as Bonnie pushed her into the passenger's side, then squirmed when she bent around her to move the seat back.

"Taking you to the hospital! You broke your damn leg, woman!"

Too tired and sore to argue, Natalie collapsed against the

seat, allowing Bonnie to gently arrange her in a less uncomfortable position. Then she watched as her girlfriend walked around the car and over to Shawn.

The two of them talked for a moment. Natalie closed her eyes, humiliated to once again be defeated by this God-forsaken Christmas dinner. A minute passed, and she fumed silently while firefighters walked back and forth from the truck to the backyard, and finally to Bonnie and Shawn, where they looked to be discussing the extent of the damage.

At one point, Shawn pointed to her, and the firefighter looked over, before heading in her direction.

Oh boy. Here we go.

"Are you the homeowner?" He leaned down slightly to make eye contact with her through the open car door. She nodded. "You're all set. It should be safe to go inside now. We turned off the kitchen appliances. Luckily, none of the damage got into the house or the foundation itself, but the back deck is no longer structurally sound. You'll want to demo and rebuild, and you'll probably want to file a claim with your insurance."

"Right..." Natalie let out a breath. She really didn't want to think about any kind of insurance right now. *At least I have insurance...* Small blessings. "Thank you for all your help. And responding so quickly..."

"We're always ready to go on holiday weekends. Yours is the fifth turkey fryer fire this year." He shook his head and chuckled to himself. "People try it every year, thinking they'll save time."

She laughed weakly. "Yeah, silly us!"

"Happy holidays, ma'am." He tilted his helmet.

"Happy holidays."

As he walked away, she slumped in the car seat. Bonnie and Shawn walked back over as the rest of the uniformed crew packed up their gear.

"I'm gonna just double-check everything to make sure it's

good. Bonnie says you need to go to the hospital? Did you get burned?"

The look on his face was one of guilt and exhaustion. Her heart broke for the guy. "No, I just put too much stress on my ankle. I think I might have made it worse. Thank you, Shawn. And really, please don't feel bad. It could have happened to any of us."

"And hey, it did!" Bonnie chimed in. Natalie shot her a look.

"Drive safe, guys. I'll call ya later, Nat."

"Okay, Shawn. Merry Christmas!"

He muttered a "Merry Christmas" back to her as he turned to head back into the house. Then Bonnie climbed into the driver's side.

Once the doors were closed and she'd turned the key, she looked at Natalie. "I just want to point out, after all of our stressing, *I* wasn't the one to ruin dinner."

Natalie sighed. "I know."

"I did good."

"Yes, honey, you did good." Natalie sunk down a little further and Bonnie reversed out the drive. "But I'd like to point out that a little extra planning *could* have maybe saved it."

She frowned at that. "Hmph."

"I really hope I don't need a cast."

THE FIREFIGHTER'S words were more prescient than Natalie gave him credit for. The emergency room was full of people with holiday-related injuries. In their corner of the waiting room alone, there was one woman with a gravy burn all up her forearm, a man who'd dislocated his shoulder while fixing a blown bulb in his lights display, and a group of neighborhood kids with potential frostbite on their fingers from an extended snowball fight.

Across the row, a group of last-minute Christmas shoppers'

hair had gotten caught in each others' ear piercings during a fight over the last unicorn pillow pet at the superstore, and the three of them had had to shuffle together awkwardly through the automatic doors, wincing and yelping as they elbowed each other in retaliation for pulling too hard against their center of gravity.

Natalie's injury was fairly low-priority. So she texted Ethan from her wheelchair, wishing him and Clara good luck in delivery. Surprisingly, he sent her a message back.

ETHAN
> 5 centimeters now. Clara's a champion. Just got the epidural.

ME
> Rooting for you two! Keep me updated.

👍

"Who're you texting?" Bonnie peeked over her shoulder.

"Ethan. Clara's close. She just got the epidural."

"God bless her," Bonnie breathed. She paused for a moment, then looked over at her girlfriend. "Do you want kids?"

"Now?" Natalie felt the blood drain from her face.

"No, of course not *now*," Bonnie said, rolling her eyes. "I mean, like, eventually. You keep saying how important family is to you. Do you want one of your own?"

Natalie thought about it for a moment. "I guess we haven't really talked about it, have we? Is that a conversation lesbians have, too?"

Natalie hadn't dated a woman seriously before Bonnie. When she'd lived in L.A., none of her relationships had ever been serious enough to merit the "do you want kids" conversation, and as she'd been on birth control for her whole adult life, she hadn't really thought about it much. She'd always been focused on work.

At least, up until she'd been fired. And since then, she'd been dealing with the house and figuring out her relationship with Bonnie. Seeing as neither one of them could get the other pregnant, she hadn't found the need to broach that topic yet.

Bonnie fiddled with her gloves in her lap. "Yeah. I mean, probably not as early on as straight couples do, I guess. I wouldn't know."

"Did you and Christel want kids?"

Natalie tried to catch her eye as she asked, but Bonnie was staring resolutely at her hands. "No. No, Christel didn't want to start a family."

"Did you?"

She realized that she was maybe taking a step too far in asking Bonnie about the dreams she'd shared, or hadn't shared, with her ex. But now that they'd broached the topic, and Natalie's half-brother and his wife were preparing to have their first child in the very same building, it seemed like the right time to bring it up.

Bonnie tilted her head, and a slight frown pulled at her lips. "No, actually. I don't think I ever did."

"Me neither." She looked up into Natalie's eyes then, and they shared a smile. Nat chuckled. "I am excited about having a little niece or nephew, though. Babies are cute. Not I-wanna-have-one-waking-me-up-four-times-a-night-to-suck-milk-outta-my-nipples cute, but cute."

Bonnie's smile turned knowing at that, and she nudged her side. "What if *I* wake you up four times a night to suck your nipples?"

Natalie smacked her on the arm. "That'd get old real fast."

"Oh come on, it could be fu–"

"Natalie Roach?" A nurse called from the central desk.

"It's Roh-ssh," Natalie corrected, and Bonnie stood so she could push her towards the nurse in her wheelchair.

"Follow me," the nurse said, ushering her over with a clipboard. Natalie wished she could just walk like normal again. She was grateful that Bonnie could wheel her around, but she was getting real tired of leaning on everyone around her. Literally.

She thought of Shawn, puttering around the house alone and likely cleaning up from dinner all by himself. Poor guy. He'd been cleaning up all of their messes this week.

The nurse dropped them off at a bed in a large open room, with curtained off sections to give patients privacy from each other in the shared emergency ward. Bonnie helped get Natalie settled while the nurse took her vitals. Once she'd made her notes in the chart and left to make her rounds, Bonnie spoke up again.

"You look like you're thinking about something. What's up?"

"Oh, just worried about Shawn," Natalie huffed. "I'm worried he's eating himself up about the fryer."

"To be fair, it was a bad idea."

The two of them shared a look. Natalie sighed and looked down at her lap, acquiescing. "Yeah, I guess it was, wasn't it?"

Bonnie put a hand on her shoulder. "You two meant well."

The doctor came in then, and just as she opened her mouth, Natalie's phone began to ring. She held up a finger and dug it out of her pocket, only to see Shawn's name appear on the screen.

She looked at Bonnie. "Can you–?"

"On it." She snatched the offered phone out of Natalie's hand and stepped out of the curtained-off area to take the call. Her voice faded as she walked away, and Natalie switched her attention to the woman in the white coat.

"Tell it to me straight, Doc. Will I ever walk again?"

CHAPTER 18

Bonnie picked up the call and wandered back out to the waiting room, hoping that she'd be able to find Natalie again once she was off the phone.

"What's up Shawn?"

A pause. "Is this Bonnie?"

"Yeah, Natalie's with the doctor right now."

"How's she doing?" His voice was laced with concern, and Bonnie considered not telling him for a fraction of a second. Then she cursed her own jealous instincts. *He's a decent guy, Bons. Stop being mean.*

"Okay, I think. It mainly only seems to hurt her when she's moving it. It's not causing her endless agony or anything."

"That's good, I guess. Can't be too serious, then?"

"We should know more in a bit once she's dealt with the doctor." Bonnie paused. "So, were you just checking in, or…?"

"Oh right! Natalie's mom is here."

Bonnie slapped a hand to her forehead. "Oh fuck. Michelle? Is she pissed?"

"Well, she ain't happy. She's got some guy with her who's got an accent, and he made some fancy dish I can't pronounce that he says needs to go in the fridge, and Nat's mom doesn't know me and thinks I'm robbing the house."

"Oh God..." Bonnie rubbed her forehead.

"I mean, I told her who I was, but now she's threatening to call the police—"

"Put her on the phone," Bonnie demanded, switching into her lawyer voice. Being obnoxious was one thing. Threatening to call the cops on Natalie's best friend was another. A short scuffling ensued as she heard Shawn walk over to Michelle and the phone switch hands.

"Who is—Natalie?? Is that you? What's going on? Why is this child at your house?"

"Hey!" Bonnie heard Shawn object, before she launched into a tirade of her own.

"Michelle, this isn't Natalie. Natalie's currently at the hospital, and I'm with her. We think she broke her leg."

"Who are you?" Michelle's tone was at once icy and exasperated. It was a timbre Bonnie recognized. Andy and Steve, her partners at the law firm, often referred to it as "Karen voice," the snooty kind of tone they'd hear from their particularly entitled clients.

"I'm Bonnie Baker. Natalie's girlfriend."

"G-girlfriend?" A long pause followed, and Bonnie refused to even acknowledge Michelle's outburst as a response. Bonnie didn't have to defend herself. "Are you still there?"

"Yes," Bonnie answered curtly. "Dinner is canceled for tonight. The man at the house is our friend, Shawn, and he has Natalie's permission to be there. He's also a contractor, so you can rest assured he's perfectly capable and qualified to take care of your daughter's house."

"I—can I just speak to my daughter, please?"

Bonnie raced out of the doors of the waiting room, as she could feel her voice rising and didn't want to disturb the other patients. "No, she's with the doctor right now. She's fine. She can call you back later."

"Well, I–"

"Goodnight, Michelle. Please pass the phone back to Shawn."

Bonnie waited as another shuffle followed, and Shawn muttered into the speaker, "I'll call you back, Bonnie."

"Got it. Sorry, Shawn, for all this, and thanks–"

And then the connection dropped.

Bonnie checked the phone screen, which had turned black, and crossed her arms over her chest to stave off the chill in the air. Just a few feet from her, paramedics were hustling to transfer a patient from an incoming emergency vehicle, and to her other side a middle-aged man was smoking a cigarette. She wiped her face with her hand and let out a breath.

She'd known that Christmas dinner would be a disaster. But this was somehow worse and better than she'd imagined. While she'd been picturing long, awkward silences around a table of judgy relatives, and hours of her trying to prove her worth as Natalie's girlfriend, what she'd gotten was an entire day of dealing with some of the hardest parts of being *anyone's* girlfriend.

Caring for an injured partner, having a huge fight, struggling with her own jealousy of friends and family, and then dealing with the aftermath when things go wrong.

She knew she ought to go back inside and be with Natalie, but she wasn't looking forward to informing her about her mom. They were both so tired, and so much of this week had been filled with stressing about everyone else in Natalie's life: Ethan, Clara, Shawn, Michelle... now, more than ever, Bonnie just wanted to have some quiet time to relax over her Christmas vacation. And with Natalie's injuries, she didn't want to be adding to her stress levels or her to-do list by telling her about Michelle's attitude.

Her eyes drifted out to the circle of asphalt that was the

emergency room drop-off. She winced at the sight of her own sedan still sitting with its blinkers on. The man on her other side snuffed out his cigarette and walked back into the waiting room, glancing only briefly over his shoulder at Bonnie. She wondered who he was waiting for. If he, like her, was just an ancillary character in someone else's life: not quite family, not quite not, struggling with his place in a maze of relationships and expectations at the holidays. Was someone near to him fighting for their life on the other side of the concrete walls? Or was he more like Ethan, on the precipice of life-changing news that he was the father of a new, healthy baby?

Or was he just some dude here for a checkup, in need of a nicotine fix?

Natalie's phone buzzed insistently, and Bonnie swiped to answer. "Hey Shawn."

"Hey Bonnie. Sorry about that. Michelle just left. Natalie still with the doctor?"

"Not sure, actually. I'm out getting some air."

"Air?" Shawn paused. "Shouldn't you be with Nat? She's probably worried about you."

"Why would she be worried about me?" Bonnie looked up at the flashing lights of her car down the concrete sidewalk.

"She's been worried about you all week!"

She tilted her head. She's *been worried about* me? "What? What do you mean?"

Shawn sighed. "She called me on Tuesday in a panic, 'cause she couldn't find the right version of Rudolph, askin' me if I had an old copy she could borrow for the two of you." He paused, and she imagined him shoving his hands in his pockets. "She specifically said it had to be the old version, too, with the original songs. She's felt awful about leaning on you too much, and earlier today when y'all fought she was all sad and worried that she'd ruined things with you. You shouldn't be leavin' her all alone in there, or she'll really think she's made you upset."

Bonnie's brow furrowed. Half the reason they'd fought today was because she'd assumed Natalie hadn't been thinking about her at all this week. Had thought that she would ruin all of Natalie's big plans.

Maybe she had it backwards. Maybe part of why Natalie hadn't wanted to ask her for help wasn't because she though Bonnie was incapable, but because she thought she was already leaning on her too much. *Did she really think she'd ruined things between us?*

She wanted to ask Shawn to tell her more, but all she could think to say was, "Really?"

"How are y'all so bad at this?" Shawn scoffed. "Seriously. Nat and I can talk about anything. Why're you two so bad at talkin' to each other?"

"We're not bad at–" Bonnie's words faltered. *Were* they bad at communicating with each other?

They were pretty good at big, long conversations. But the longer she thought about it, she realized that she *did* hide a lot of her real feelings from Natalie. She was afraid that if she shared too much, she might scare her away. She liked talking to Natalie about *her* feelings. But the more she thought about it, the more she realized she wasn't as good about talking to her about her own.

The irony of Shawn being the one telling her all of this, when his and Nat's friendship was one of the things she'd been insecure about since they'd started dating, didn't escape her either.

"She made you get a copy of the old Rudolph?" She said instead, her stomach twisting. That was one of the few family memories she *had* told Natalie. And it had been important enough to her that she'd enlisted Shawn's help in making it something they could share together.

Shawn let out a breath. She could practically hear his eye roll as he answered, "Yes. I left it under the tree for you. Now I'm going home for the night; the kitchen and everything seems to be fine. Just don't use the back door until I fix up the deck, okay?"

Bonnie smiled. Maybe she'd misjudged the poor guy. "Okay. And Shawn?"

"Yeah?"

"Thanks for taking care of our girl. I'm gonna go in there and make sure she's doing okay."

"'Bout time," Shawn muttered. "Merry Christmas, Bonnie."

"Merry Christmas, Shawn."

Bonnie hung up the call and tucked the phone into her jacket pocket. She was about to head back inside when a bright red tow truck pulled into the drop-off circle. Her heart leapt to her throat as she saw it approach her sedan.

"Wait! Stop! I'll move it, I'll move it!" Bonnie yelled, as she ran as fast as she could in her kitten heels to the other side of the entrance. "Don't tow it!"

A grumpy-looking man with salt-and-pepper scruff covering his chin grunted at her as she approached. He was already writing out an impound ticket. "This your car?" He drawled.

"Yes, yes, and I can move it, I'm so sorry," she panted. He grunted again.

"No can do, lady. Once I'm called, it's my job to take it to the lot. Otherwise, I don't get paid."

"How much are they paying you?"

He looked up from his ticket book and raised an eyebrow. "Excuse me?"

"I'll double it."

"It's a holiday, lady. It's time-and-a-half. You got that kinda cash?" He eyed her up and down.

She fought the urge to roll her eyes at him. "Look, my uh–" her mind drew a blank as she realized she didn't want to give this guy any reason not to like her. If he told this redneck that she needed her car to drive her *girlfriend* home at the end of the night, he might tow it away just out of spite.

Every fiber of her being fought against the next words that came out of her mouth. "My sister's in there, and we just had the worst family dinner of our life. The turkey fryer exploded on her, she broke her leg while trying to put out the fire, and on top of it all, her mom's blaming it all on her!"

"*Her* mom? Don't you and your sister have the same mother?"

Bonnie winced. "We're half-sisters."

"Huh." He went back to writing his ticket.

"Please!" Bonnie practically threw herself between him and the car. The smell of stale cigarette smoke and laundry detergent wafted over her as she squeezed between them. "It'll completely ruin our Christmas if we have to get the car out of the pound tonight, too."

"Look, lady, I feel for ya, I do, but you're blocking emergency traffic."

"And I'm gonna move it!" Bonnie's exclamation approached a shriek. She swallowed, and evened her tone. "Lemme make it up to you. Seriously. What are they paying you?"

"$300."

What is it with this Christmas and everything being three hundred dollars?

Then a stroke of inspiration flashed through her mind brighter than Rudolph's shining nose cut through the Christmas Eve fog.

"I'll pay you six if you let me move my car now, and I'll even throw in another job for you the day after Christmas."

"Six? For two jobs?" He threw up his hands.

"Eight! No—an even grand!"

He looked her up and down, frowning. "You're bluffing."

"I'll write you a check right now," she said, opening the driver's door and pulling her checkbook out from the glove box. "What's your name?"

"Ernie."

"Ernie...?"

"White." His face turned incredulous as he watched her write the check. "You're seriously giving me a thousand dollars just to let you off the hook?"

"Yes," Bonnie answered shamelessly. She finished scribbling the amount and Natalie's address on the paper and ripped it off its serrated edge. "And meet me at that address there on the 26th. I've got a Christmas delivery I need to make."

Ernie eyed the piece of paper cautiously. "A Christmas delivery, huh?"

"Yep."

He folded up the check and reached out his hand. "Alright, ma'am. You got yourself a deal."

They shook on it.

AFTER SHE'D MOVED her car to the appropriate lot and transferred the right amount of money over to her checking account, she rushed back into the hospital to look for Natalie. Unfortunately, once she made it to the patient intake, she realized they'd moved her somewhere else.

"Excuse me?" She approached the security desk.

A woman in a dark blue uniform looked up to greet her. "Are you here with a patient?"

"Yes. Natalie Roche?"

The woman directed Bonnie to fill out a check-in sheet on a clipboard while she looked her up. "It looks like she was taken away for X-rays. You can have a seat over there, we'll call you over when she gets back."

With a sigh, she returned to the waiting area in the hopes that she'd be able to reunite with Natalie soon. *At least I'll be able to tell her I have good news.*

CHAPTER 19

When the doctor said they'd need to take Natalie to another room for X-rays, she tried to delay them as much as possible to give Bonnie time. But eventually, they'd told her that she was holding up the other patients.

Without her phone, she had no way of contacting her. But now that she was at least in a doctor's care, someone would be able to help Bonnie find her, she figured.

And her leg really hurt.

A few hours later, her leg was set in a hard cast for a stress fracture that was only slightly more serious than the one she'd been treated for at Urgent Care earlier that week. They'd wheeled her back to the same bed she'd been assigned to earlier, only this time she didn't have Bonnie with her. Or her phone.

The minutes dragged on without anything to keep her occupied. The other patients around her were in worse shape than she was, but most of them had family to talk to. At first, she was confused as to what was taking Bonnie so long. Surely she would have found her by now if she was looking.

But after half an hour of checking the clock repeatedly and making up elaborate stories in her mind of how everyone had landed themselves into the beds beside her, she just got bored. Then antsy.

She peeked around the room. No one was paying even the slightest bit of attention to the short, white woman in the wheelchair. Testing the waters, she wheeled forward about a foot past her bed to see if anyone noticed.

Nope.

Before she knew it, she'd traveled all the way across the emergency room and arrived at the end of the corridor, where a directory was posted by the double doors. Natalie perused the list.

"Labor and Delivery" was on the fourth floor.

Happy to have a direction, Natalie slipped onto the elevator and made her way to find her family.

"Excuse me," Natalie rung the bell at the nurses' station in the entrance of Labor and Delivery. This floor was much less hectic than the one she'd just left, and she was grateful for the relative quiet. A red-headed nurse answered the call, and asked Natalie what she needed.

"My sister-in-law arrived a few hours ago. I was hoping I could visit her?"

"What's the name?"

"Clara Espinoza."

Natalie waited patiently while the woman looked at her computer.

"It looks like she's still in delivery. You can wait here for her if you want." The nurse rose from her chair and gestured for Natalie to follow her. They wandered through a locked set of doors and over to another waiting area, which, once again, felt much more welcoming than the one she'd just left.

"Thanks so much."

Magazines, children's books, and a few toys that Natalie had only ever seen in doctor's offices and waiting rooms littered the various tables in between the wide wood-and-pleather chairs throughout the space. The two televisions that hung on the walls were tuned to the local news, where the broadcasters were lamenting about an approaching cold front.

She wove through the rows for a few moments, paused to leaf through a magazine or two, before she found herself getting bored again. *What did people even do in the age before phones?*

"No–please–I'm sorry, I can handle it! Let me back in there!"

"Sir, it's okay. Take a moment, we'll come and get you after you've had a snack and settled down."

Natalie looked up at the sound of Ethan's voice and someone she hadn't heard before. A man in a mask and scrubs had a grip on Ethan's arm. He stopped briefly by the nurse's station, spoke with the attending there, and then led Ethan over to the chairs before handing him a granola bar and a juicebox.

"It's very common for loved ones to get light-headed in the delivery room. Please eat a little something and then I'll send someone out to get you."

"But Clara–"

"She'll be just fine, I assure you." The nurse gave him a reassuring smile. Ethan, who was looking quite pale, swallowed.

"If you need anything else, just ask Gerda at the nurse's station."

He gestured behind him, before giving Ethan another nod and a smile and turning his heel to return to the delivery room.

Ethan shoved a hand through his thinning hair and let out a breath. Then he unwrapped a little plastic straw and stabbed it into his juice box.

"Ethan?" Natalie was torn between feeling worried for her brother and grateful for the company. "Is Clara okay?"

"Oh, *she's* fine. I'm the one that can't seem to handle the miracle of childbirth." He shook his head, and she watched as a shiver worked its way down his spine. "It's terrifying. Did you know about all the stuff that comes out?"

Natalie winced, remembering the movie they'd had all the kids watch back in health class. "I've heard it can be a lot."

"I've never seen her like that. And the *cursing*." Ethan took a sip of his juice. "Why doesn't anyone tell you what to expect?? She's never talked like that before."

"So they're making you wait out here because...?"

He closed his eyes in embarrassment. "I may have... passed out for a second. When I walked around the bed to get Clara some ice, I happened to peek at what the Doctor was looking at, and..." His breath hitched and his face went a little green. "Uh, well. Then one of the nurses brought me out here. Gave me some juice."

He held up his tiny juicebox and his granola bar.

"Would you like something a little more substantial? We could go to the cafeteria for a second."

Ethan looked at her as if really seeing her for the first time. "Wait a minute–what are you even doing up here? Why are you in a gown?"

She stuck out her tongue. "I hurt my leg when I tossed the cooler at the grease fire. I already had a hairline fracture in my tibia, and apparently I made it worse."

Ethan shook his head. "We're kinda bad at this whole Christmas dinner thing, aren't we?"

"Yeah, let's try not to make *this* a tradition," she said, gesturing first to her leg, and then to the hospital around them. "Something tells me this isn't what Grandma had in mind when she said she wanted us all to get along."

He chuckled, and Natalie smiled as some of the color returned to his face. "Yeah. There are better ways to spend the holidays. I like presents."

She laughed. "I guess next year, there will be a little baby to buy presents for."

And just like that, the color drained from his cheeks again.

"Ethan? You okay? Stay with me, buddy." She wheeled closer and grabbed hold of his wrist, checking for a pulse. He shook his head and waved her away.

"I'm fine, I'm fine... I really should get back in there."

He started to get up, and Natalie leaned forward to push him back into his seat. "Absolutely not! You're still white as a sheet! Eat your cookie."

"It's a granola bar," he grumbled. She scowled at him. "Fine."

She eyed him as he unwrapped the snack, the paper crinkling throughout the quiet waiting room. "So... you're gonna be a dad."

He took a bite. Mouth still full, he answered, "And you're gonna be an aunt."

Heat rose to her cheeks. "Yeah. I guess I am. How–how do you feel about that?"

"About being a dad?"

"About... me. Being Aunt Natalie."

He chewed thoughtfully. "I think it'll be good. She's going to have a strong mom, and grandmother... the more female role models she has in her life, the better."

"It's gonna be a girl??" Natalie sucked in a breath. This is the first she'd heard that. Ethan nodded.

"Clara didn't want to tell anyone. We've been trying to keep the whole gender thing pretty neutral, just cause..." He looked over at her and shrugged. "I don't know. It's not good to shove that down any kid's throat nowadays, you know?"

Warmth spread through her chest as a smile took over her face. *I had no idea that they'd be so progressive.* "I do. That's awesome. Good for you."

"But we still picked girl names," he insisted.

Her smile didn't falter. "What did you pick?"

"Sofia." He got a faraway look in his eyes, and he played with the wrapper in his lap. "Sofia Liliana Espinoza."

Natalie had never felt emotional when talking about babies. But the way her brother's eyes sparkled as he said his daughter's name, so close to their own grandmother's name, and the misty expression on his face, was enough to make her blink back a couple of tears that threatened to fall. "That's beautiful, Ethan."

He smiled and looked down at his hands, before tilting his head back to his sister. "And what should she call you? Just Natalie? Auntie?"

"Ooo, I *do* like Auntie."

"Auntie Natalie." He took another sip from his juicebox. He *was* looking quite a bit better than he was when he'd first been dragged into the waiting room. "And what about Bonnie?"

"Bonnie?" She blinked, then looked away. "Eh, it might be a little early to pick out a name for Bonnie."

She still hadn't returned from her phone call with Shawn. Natalie was beginning to wonder if she'd abandoned her entirely.

Ethan frowned slightly, then bumped her elbow. "Think about it. Like I said, she's gonna need some strong female role models."

The tears that had she'd fought back earlier returned. "I will. Thanks, Ethan."

"You bet."

"Mr. Espinoza?" The nurse had returned. "She's asking for you. How are you feeling?"

"Better, thank you." He rose as he approached and looked back at Natalie. "I'll let you know how it goes."

"Good luck, Dad."

She waved at him as he looked back over his shoulder one more time, before rounding the corner to join his wife.

And once again, Natalie was alone.

CHAPTER 20

Bonnie had lost her.
She'd waited for hours before she'd finally gone up to the nurse's station to see if there'd been any update on Natalie. Turns out, she'd been out of X-rays for half of that time and they'd forgotten to let her know.

But when she went back to her bed in the Emergency Ward, Natalie was nowhere to be found.

At first, she walked through the rest of the ward, attempting not to look to snoopy as she peaked around the curtains for signs of her wheelchair-bound girlfriend. Then she doubled back along the hallway where she'd left to take Shawn's phone call. Along the way, she peeked through the windows lining the corridors to see if maybe she'd snuck into someone's room.

But Natalie was gone. She walked back to the nurse's station.

"Um... my girlfriend's not at her bed?"

Whereas before, the woman had hardly looked Bonnie's way before waving her through to the shared ward, this time she looked her straight into her eyes. She wore a slightly annoyed expression. "Who's your girlfriend again?"

"Natalie Roche."

"Roche... Roe-shh... Can you spell that?"

They sorted out the spelling and after another search, the woman at the desk asked a passing nurse in lavender scrubs if she'd seen a woman in a wheelchair pass by.

"What does she look like?" the nurse asked shortly. Bonnie shuffled her feet as attention shifted back to her. She felt like she was in trouble.

"Brown hair, on the shorter side. Um..." The nurse tapped her foot expectantly. "White. Curvy. Leg likely propped up?"

"I did see a woman wheel past the station earlier. She's probably just in the bathroom. I'm sure she'll be back in a minute."

Bonnie breathed a sigh of relief. "Thank you. You're right, she's probably back by now."

Bonnie returned to the bed, but it was still empty. Ten minutes later, she still hadn't returned.

The longer she waited, the more nervous she became. Blood rushed in her ears, and Shawn's words echoed in her head. *She's probably worried about you...* Oh God. Had Natalie gone looking for her? She still had Natalie's phone. *What was I thinking, taking so long with the car?*

Bonnie sped-walked to the nurse's station again. The secretary from earlier was behind the desk and almost completely obscured by a stack of paperwork. "Um... I'm sorry to bother you again, but my girlfriend still hasn't returned to her bed, and she was brought back from X-rays over an hour ago. Is there any chance she got lost?"

"Name?"

Bonnie held back a groan as she gritted through the same questions she'd been asked three times since returning from the parking lot and the woman typed them into her computer. Finally, she gave a decisive nod and picked up the phone. "We'll put out a call with security."

"I can help look!" Bonnie jumped at the chance to take action. "Maybe she went looking for her brother and sister-in-law. They were admitted earlier this evening."

The woman hung up the phone with a loud clatter, rolling her eyes to the ceiling before swinging back around to her desktop. "Why didn't you say so earlier? What are their names?"

BONNIE CHECKED her watch as she rode the elevator to the fourth floor, and jumped when she realized it was past midnight. After almost another hour of waiting for security to search, she'd decided to just search for Natalie herself. She'd followed the green arrows on the floor and a few directory signs, and at last was on her way up to Labor and Delivery.

She found her way to the nurse's station, rung the bell, and was directed to another hallway, where she had to be badged in. She explained the situation to *another* secretary, and they let her through.

Jeez, I get they need to be secure, but for goodness' sake... Bonnie found herself taking quick steps as she explored the wide hallways. She'd been so intent on making it through the various sections that she almost missed the brunette in the wheelchair who was looking in through a large window down the corridor to her right.

"Natalie??"

Bonnie stopped abruptly, her flats slipping on the waxed floor a little as she scrambled to pivot directions. At the end of the hall, Natalie looked over to her and smiled.

"Have you been here the whole time?" Bonnie jogged up to her.

Natalie ignored her question. Instead, she turned her chair to face her, pointing through the glass at one of the bassinets in the clean, white room. Her eyes were filled with wonder in a way Bonnie had never seen before.

"See the one that's two from the end there, Bons? In the little yellow knit cap?"

Bonnie followed her finger. "They've all got yellow knit caps, hon."

"Yeah, but you see her, right?" Natalie wiggled her finger insistently through the glass.

Bonnie looked again, counted two babies from the end, and landed on a tiny, wrinkly thing that was wailing its little heart out. Its itty-bitty feet were waving back and forth, and the beanie on its head twisted as it turned its neck side to side.

"Yeah, I see her." Bonnie's tone was impartial, but the longer she stared, the more the little thing started to win her over. She didn't stop moving. Her arms waved back and forth, and her feet bounced up and down underneath her little blanket.

Bonnie looked over to the woman beside her and saw her eyes glistening. A dumb, goofy grin plastered across her face. "Are you absolutely sure you don't want kids?"

"Nah, I'm content being an Auntie. To that little girl. Right there."

"What's her name?"

"Sofia Espinoza. Seven pounds, three ounces."

"She's beautiful," Bonnie said, in part because that's just what people say in these situations. But then the tiny thing screamed out loud enough to attract the attention of the attendant in the nursery, and she shook her itty bitty pink fists as she approached. An involuntary smile tugged at Bonnie's lips. "Congratulations."

"Ethan asked what she should call you."

"Me?" Bonnie straightened in surprise.

"Yeah," Natalie said, giving her the side-eye. "Are you an Auntie Bonnie?"

Bonnie flinched. "I might not be Auntie anything once I tell you how I yelled at your mom."

Natalie blinked. "Mom? *Mom!*" She slapped a hand to her

forehead. "Oh my God, I completely forgot about mom! Fuck, she must be furious—"

"She was. She called." Bonnie pulled Natalie's phone out of her back pocket and handed it back to her. "Apparently, Shawn was still there when she got to the house. The smoke has settled down, by the way."

"Oh no..." If it weren't for the wheelchair, she looked as if she would have fallen right to the floor in embarrassment. She checked the screen, then hung her face into her hands. "What did she say?"

"Oh, she was pissed." Bonnie grabbed hold of the handles of her wheelchair and started to push her back towards the elevator. "Couldn't believe how inconsiderate you were not to let her know. She was so mad that she didn't even realize I wasn't you until I told her to calm down."

"Don't tell me—"

"Well she asked who I was."

"What did you say?"

"That I was Bonnie Baker, Esquire. Your lawyer."

Natalie whipped her head around. "You didn't!"

Bonnie grinned in spite of herself. "No, of course not. I said I was your girlfriend. Honestly, though, it had a similar effect to the lawyer line. Shut her right up."

Natalie faced forward once more and slouched back. "So now she knows..." They stopped moving. The chair jerked slightly as Bonnie raised her hands to her lips.

"Oh my God, Nat, I'm so sorry." Bonnie rushed around in front of the chair and kneeled until she was level with her. "I outed you to your mom."

"It's fine, hon—"

"No, no it isn't." Bonnie shook her head vehemently, eyes pleading. "I am so, so sorry, honey. That was not my place. I just couldn't believe the audacity of Michelle, when your home was literally smoking from a grease fire, and you're *in the hospital*, to be upset about such a silly thing like Christmas dinner. I didn't even think–"

"Bons!" Natalie leaned forward and placed her hands on Bonnie's shoulders. "Seriously. It's okay."

"Are you sure?" Tears threatened to fall from Bonnie's eyes. "I know you hadn't told her yet because you were waiting for the right time, and…"

Natalie nodded, eyes drifting away as she got lost in thought. Bonnie had been so worried about Natalie, that she'd completely forgotten about the whole reason she'd wanted Michelle to come to Christmas dinner in the first place. Natalie had told her that she'd wanted to introduce her to her mom. To come out, officially.

Bonnie had ruined it. After all had fallen apart: the menu, the fire, the hospital… all things that hadn't been Bonnie's fault, she'd still managed to fuck up the most important thing.

"Will you ever forgive me?"

Natalie's eyes snapped back to Bonnie's face. "So you're saying she called my phone, angry I hadn't gotten in touch with her, when she could see the house literally smoking in front of her?"

Bonnie let out a breath. "Yeah."

"And she yelled at Shawn?"

Bonnie choked on a giggle. "Yeah."

Natalie nodded. "There's nothing to forgive, Bons. Like you said: she'll either love me, or she won't. Nothing I can do will change that."

"Thank you for taking the call."

"You're sure you're not mad?"

Natalie shook her head. "Honestly? I'm tired. Tired of trying to impress her. Ethan and I aren't perfect, by far, but we're both trying to make it work. We're being honest with each other about how awkward it is, yet... he understands that I want to make things right. And I think he's open to that. He even said that he wanted me to be in Sofia's life. Mom, on the other hand..." Bonnie winced as she shifted on her knees in front of her. Natalie waved at her. "Jesus, honey, stand up! We can talk and roll."

"Oh thank God," Bonnie groaned as she straightened, knee popping. "My legs might not be broken, but I'm not a young woman anymore."

"You're plenty young," Natalie argued. Then she took a deep breath and continued. "I still feel like I'm trying to impress my mom, Bons. And the truth is, I shouldn't have to, should I?"

Bonnie didn't even hesitate. "No. No you shouldn't."

"I'm gay."

"Yep."

"I have a girlfriend."

"Sure do," Bonnie agreed.

"And..." Natalie leaned her head back and looked at her girlfriend, who'd retaken control of her chair. "She's either going to accept that, or she isn't."

A security officer waved them over and Bonnie wheeled them in his direction. She recognized him as one of the group who'd been sent to look for Natalie in the first place. They followed him into the elevator, where he pressed the button for the ground floor. They were quiet for a second, and then Bonnie broke the silence.

"I can't believe I'm saying this," she started, "But give her a few days. She was taken off-guard today. She might come around. Who knows?"

Natalie turned around fully in her chair, twisting her spine. "Bonnie Louise Baker, did you honestly just express some kind of hope that a parent might do the right thing? You're not getting sentimental, are you?"

"I know, I know." Bonnie snorted. "Don't get used to it."

The elevator opened, and they moved forward and out of the way of an oncoming gurney.

"But, just so I know... what makes you say that?" Natalie's voice was quiet enough that Bonnie almost didn't hear her over the ruckus of the hospital floor.

Bonnie shrugged. She wasn't even entirely sure what had caused her to think Michelle might turn around. But at the same time... "She's been trying to get to know you again. Trust me, I'm the first to say I think she's misguided about a lot of things, but... she's at least been trying. And she's stubborn. Maybe she won't want to throw away all of the work you two have done just yet."

Natalie hummed. "Maybe."

"And I did tell her to watch out because I was a lawyer," Bonnie teased.

"Bonnie!"

"What?" At last, they found the bed that she'd abandoned earlier that evening. "Don't all moms just want their daughters to settle down with an attractive lawyer?"

"No, I'm pretty sure they prefer doctors," Natalie quipped.

"Well, you're not going to win over any doctors if you run away from your bed without clearance first." Doctor Pollard tapped her painted fingernails on Natalie's chart. She didn't look happy about security being called to locate her runaway patient. Her mouth was set in a stern frown as Bonnie pushed Natalie forward. "Miss Roche."

At least they had the good sense to look guilty.

"Dr. Pollard. Sorry. My brother just had a baby upstairs."

"Well that *is* quite unusual."

The three of them were quiet a moment, and then a wheeze sounded from the bed next to them. "Good one, Doc!"

"Thank you, Harold." She turned to them again. "Get it? Because typically, men don't go into labor?"

Natalie and Bonnie leaned their heads back simultaneously

in understanding. "Oooooh!" Too late, they forced out some unconvincing laughs.

"The moment's passed, ladies. Congratulations," she added to Natalie. "Let's get your paperwork squared away so you can go home."

CHAPTER 21

Christmas Eve dawned bright and cold, with a light snow drifting lazily through the air. And Natalie and Bonnie slept right through it.

Exhausted, the pair didn't rise until noon, when at last Bonnie wrenched her eyes open to the sunlight pouring in through the upstairs window.

To be honest, she didn't even remember how she and Natalie had navigated the stairs the night before. Though she assumed they hadn't used the crutch when she executed a cursory glance around the bedroom and saw no sign of it.

Alright, well. We can fix that.

She tossed the covers off her side of the bed, slapping Natalie in the face with the comforter.

"Mmm," she muttered, as the bed creaked under Bonnie's shifting weight. "'S'morning already?"

"It's afternoon." Bonnie rubbed her eyes.

"What? No. I don't believe it."

"Believe it, gorgeous. We slept through breakfast."

"And coffee?"

Bonnie grinned at the pure, child-like terror that laced

Natalie's whining voice. She chuckled. "No, no, I can make us coffee. You stay here. I'll get your crutch."

Natalie rolled over in response. Bonnie set about the morning tasks, recovering the crutch from the kitchen downstairs and starting the coffee, brushing her teeth and electing to throw on a bathrobe instead of getting fully dressed. While the coffee brewed, she checked her phone to see what restaurants delivered on Christmas Eve, and how early they closed.

She wasn't even ready to *think* about cooking again.

She checked the weather. It looked as if the weather reports from the night before were coming true: they were calling for one to three inches of snow that night, and the I-81 corridor was keeping its fingers crossed for a White Christmas.

She checked the fridge to make sure that they had enough food to get them through a few days, and was shocked to find a dome of meringue staring back at her. She blinked.

Fifteen minutes later, Natalie loped into the kitchen, wincing as the pad of her crutch jutted into her armpit. Bonnie was just pulling the baked alaska out of the oven. "I smell coffee."

"I told you I'd make some. And look, we even have something special for breakfast."

"What?"

Bonnie plopped the dessert on the counter. "Voila!"

Natalie stared at her. "Oh my God. How did it not melt? Hasn't it been in there overnight?"

She shrugged and placed it on the table, then grabbed a knife to cut into it. "It was in the fridge. Let's see how it did."

Natalie poured the coffee as Bonnie sunk the knife through the meringue, only to hit a hard wall of dry ice. Instantly, smoke began to billow from the cut.

"You've got to be kidding me..."

Natalie plunked the mugs on the table. "There's no way the ice cream is still frozen."

"Not the ice cream. *The dry ice.*"

"*What?*" Natalie sunk into a chair and pulled the smoking dish closer to her. "You're kidding."

Bonnie handed her the knife, and she used it to poke at the meringue, gingerly peeling back a layer without touching it with her hands.

"I can't believe this..."

"You have to text Shawn," Bonnie said, shaking her head in disbelief.

Natalie set the knife down and dug her phone out of her bathrobe pocket. She narrated as she typed in the message. "You'll... never... believe... what's... still... frozen..."

Bonnie scraped at the layer of ice beneath the meringue, which was now peeling away from the edges of its own volition as the carbon dioxide sublimated beneath it. "Even the ice cream is frozen solid."

"Well," Natalie sipped at her coffee, "At least it didn't melt this time."

"It's a Christmas miracle!"

LATER THAT NIGHT, the two of them snuggled up as cozy as they could with Natalie's bulky cast propped on the arm of the couch. The tree was at last decorated with ornaments from both Natalie's and Bonnie's collection: an eclectic mix of pop-culture novelty ornaments, dollar store baubles, and some of Sophie Roche's antique glass balls that they'd insisted on hanging in the best spots. Just as Bonnie had settled underneath Natalie's legs, she smacked a hand to her forehead.

"Oh shoot! I almost forgot! Your Christmas present!"

"It's not Christmas yet," Bonnie moaned. "Nat, I just sat down. Let's just find a cheesy movie on Netflix and—"

"No, this is important! Please, honey? It's in the hall closet, in a red bag."

"Okaaay..."

Bonnie lifted her girlfriend's legs off of her lap and collected the gift from the hall closet. While she was there, she also pulled out the giant Santa bag filled with baby clothes for Ethan and Clara and the wine Natalie had bought for her mother and set them under the tree.

"Aww. Those look nice." Nat's smile faltered a bit at seeing the box that held the wine.

"Don't think too hard about it, hon. If things are still weird with Michelle, we'll just drink her present instead."

A wry laugh slipped from her as she took a sip of the wine they'd poured to go with the takeout that was due to arrive any minute. It was still relatively early, only around 5:00, but the sun had already begun to set outside the window, which made the glow from the woodstove and the bubble lights feel even warmer.

"Alright. Open your present."

"I feel bad, I don't have anything for you to open." Bonnie grabbed her gift bag and plopped back onto the couch, careful to avoid hitting the cast. "But I do have a surprise. And I think you'll like it."

"Yours first, though."

Bonnie's eyes sparkled as she shot her a look, then ripped the tissue paper out of her bag. Inside was a shipping box that had clearly been opened already and re-sealed with scotch tape.

She peeled it open, and pulled out a tiny, white ceramic farmhouse, with painted yellow windows and a red door, and a little green wreath detailed in the center. Along the roofline, there was a message inscribed: *Our First Christmas Together, 20xx.*

A red ribbon poked out of the top, and Bonnie held it by the loop, only to realize–

"It's an ornament."

Natalie nodded, gauging her reaction. "For our tree. That we can always decorate together."

Bonnie's throat tightened as she adjusted her grip on the tiny house. "I love it. Can I hang it?"

"There's still a spot, right in the middle." She pointed at the one branch they hadn't yet weight down with anything. Bonnie carried it over and secured it on a branch, where its shiny glaze reflected the lights of the tree.

"Thank you, honey."

"Merry Christmas, Bonnie."

They smiled at each other, then she stepped back to admire their happy tree and set the red gift bag back underneath. As she bent down, she tripped backwards at the sight of a pair of beady eyes staring back at her under the branches.

"Jesus! What the—"

"What is it?" Natalie yelped.

Bonnie cautiously crawled back to the tree and lifted the branches...

Only to see Shawn's fucking Elf-on-the-Shelf sitting on top of a battered VHS copy of Rudolph the Red-Nosed Reindeer.

"I am going to kill him, Natalie. I swear." She snatched up the stuffed toy and the VHS and carried them both back to the couch. "And he didn't even bring us a DVD! So we can't even watch it!"

"Sure we can!" Natalie pointed at end table next to the mantel, where her laptop sat on top of a—

Well, I'll be. It was an old VCR.

"I wasn't about to throw out Grandma's VCR when I was sure there would be some home movies floating around here somewhere." Natalie grabbed the Elf from where Bonnie had tossed it. "I haven't found them yet, but I'm sure they're in one of the many boxes I've yet to go through. We have to get Shawn back with this somehow."

An idea sparked in Bonnie's mind. "I know exactly how we can get back at him!"

But at that moment, the doorbell rang. Bonnie hopped to the kitchen to grab her wallet and answered the door, where their Chinese food was waiting.

"Thank you so much!" She called to the delivery driver as they dashed down the driveway, which was still just barely visible under a thickening layer of snow. Hands full of double-orders of their favorite dishes, she returned to the living room, where Natalie was doing her best to sit up and clear the coffee table.

"I got it, I got it. You lay still for once," Bonnie snapped, waving her away. "You're injured. Let me take care of you."

"You always take care of me." Natalie wiggled her eyebrows suggestively as she leaned back into the couch cushions.

"Mm. Well, maybe that'll be another one of your Christmas presents. But for now, we feast!"

She divvied out plates of crab lo mein and General Tso's, and once Natalie had her dinner balanced on her lap, she grabbed the VHS and carried it over to the VCR. "Now, does the TV have to be on channel three for this thing to work, or is it just an input switch?"

"Umm..."

It took them a little longer than either of them would like to admit, but eventually, they figured out the VCR. And the two of them snuggled up to spend their first Christmas Eve together decorating the tree, eating Chinese take-out, and watching the original Rankin and Bass Rudolph the Red-Nosed Reindeer.

CHAPTER 22

On Christmas Day, a heaping inch of snow just covered the grass across Natalie Roche's street in rural Maryland.

After a rather exhausting hour navigating how to wrap Natalie's cast in plastic so she could take a shower, the two of them decided to spend the rest of the day lounging about in their pajamas.

The TV was tuned to the Hallmark Channel, where frame after frame of cheesy plot lines played out by unnaturally attractive actors scrolled past, with the volume turned low enough so that they didn't have to shout their commentary. They munched on leftover fried rice and scalloped potatoes (the one dish from the Christmas dinner that hadn't been completely destroyed), and decided to forego the coffee in lieu of some hot chocolate spiked with peppermint schnapps.

At some point in the afternoon, the doorbell rang.

"Carolers?" Natalie perked up, stretching her neck to spy through the living room window from the couch.

"I don't hear any singing." Since Bonnie had already snapped at Natalie for conspiring to wear out her crutch, she got up to go check the front door.

An older woman with bleached blonde curls stood under the overhang, with a tall, tan dark-haired man beside her.

"Hello?" Bonnie was glad she'd thought to pull her bathrobe on over her pajamas before answering the door. "How can I help you?"

"You must be Natalie's girlfriend!" The man said, sticking out his hand. "I am Rafael. It is so nice to meet you."

"Uhh… hi." She shook his hand. "What are–?" It was then that Bonnie realized who was standing in front of her. "Michelle. Rafael. What a surprise!"

She pulled her robe tighter. Unsure of what to do, she simply stared at the couple for a moment, before figuring that it couldn't really get any more awkward than it already was. "Come in."

"Thank you. Bonnie, was it?" Michelle slipped inside and paused to wipe her expensive boots on the doormat. "So this is the inside. My goodness, it's been years. It's like stepping back in time…"

"A gift for you, and for Natalie." Rafael shoved a tall, round, foil-wrapped dish into Bonnie's arms.

"Oh, th-thank you, Rafael." Hands now full, she found herself quite grateful when Natalie hobbled into the foyer.

"What's all–mom!" Her eyes widened, and darted from Michelle to Rafael to Bonnie. "We weren't expecting you."

"I know, honey. I'm sorry for arriving unexpectedly. We won't stay long. I just wanted to make sure we were able to drop off a special Christmas pudding Rafael prepared for you, since we weren't able to enjoy it on Saturday." Her tone was somewhere between regretful and disciplinary, as if the two women had disappointed her, but she was willing to give them a second chance. Then she sniffed the air. "I'm happy to see it doesn't smell like smoke in here."

"Your leg, Natalie, does it hurt? Please sit, do not stand for us." Rafael gestured down the hall to the kitchen, and Natalie nodded graciously, taking his lead.

"Why don't we all sit for a minute? We actually just had lunch and were about to make some coffee, weren't we, Bons?"

"Yes! Of course," Bonnie said, picking up on her improvisation. "Would you like to join us?"

"That would be lovely, thank you."

As they shuffled into the kitchen, Bonnie placed Rafael's present onto the table on her way to the counter. She went about brewing a pot of coffee while Natalie entertained her mother as if it were a completely normal thing to stop by someone's house unannounced, after a fight, on a holiday.

"How's your Christmas been, Mom?"

"Lovely. Just a quiet few days at home. Rafael closed the restaurant for the weekend, so we've actually been able to relax together for once."

She reached for the man's hand, and he beamed at her. *They're actually kinda sweet,* Bonnie mused, keeping an eye on Natalie's reaction, *even if the age difference is a little much.* She decided to follow her girlfriend's lead in this situation. If she wanted to play hostess, Bonnie would break out the coffee and the dessert forks. But if things got testy, she was ready to help her toss them out in the snow in a second.

"I made special dessert!" Rafael suddenly switched from his intimate smile to a grin that brightened his whole face. "For the family! Do you have bowls?"

"Here." Bonnie reached for the pile of paper products they'd hoarded in preparation for the dinner that never was. She passed out plasticware and plates around the table, then went about to gather mugs for the coffee as he unpeeled the foil from the container.

"It is new to me–baked alaska!"

She almost dropped Natalie's coffee as she turned around,

slack-jawed, as he revealed a beautifully piped dome of meringue, perfectly browned, atop a delicately iced layer cake with chocolate and caramel shards picked around the base.

"It's... beautiful," Natalie breathed. She put a hand to her mouth.

Bonnie wondered for a moment if she was stifling a laugh.

"I had mentioned it to him in passing while talking about some of the crazier things we used to make for dinner parties back in the 70's, but we *never* made something this delightful. Dark Chocolate and Salted Caramel, with just the lightest angel food cake you've ever had in your life–"

"And a hint of lime in the buttercream," he added.

Bonnie gathered herself and finished passing out the coffee. She and Natalie shared a look. "Well, I, for one, can't wait to try it."

CONSIDERING the disastrous phone call that Bonnie had described to Natalie in the hospital less than 48 hours earlier, the rest of Michelle's impromptu visit went surprisingly well. The conversation was light, but pleasant, and Rafael was a delight. Not only was he the one to help keep the conversation moving when things got stilted, his baked alaska may have been the most delicious thing Natalie had ever tasted.

Most importantly, he seemed to bring out a new side to her mother: for the first time in years, Natalie was pretty sure that she saw genuine happiness sparkle in her eyes. She wondered if he was actually the reason they'd come to visit in the first place; perhaps he was part of the reason Michelle had been trying, in her own way, to be part of Natalie's life again.

About an hour after the plates had been cleared and the last drips of coffee had been drunk, Bonnie looked over towards her. She nodded, and then turned to her mom.

"I actually have a gift for you too, Mom, if Bonnie could help me out..."

"On it!" Bonnie hopped up from the table like she'd been doing all evening, only this time she returned with the gift back that Natalie had prepared.

"They're some of my favorites from California," Natalie explained as Michelle unwrapped them. "I had a couple cases in my apartment out there that I'd forgotten about until I finished unpacking the moving pod. I couldn't remember if you preferred red or white..."

"This is lovely, Natalie. Thank you." Michelle reached a hand across the table and squeezed Natalie's fingers. Then she turned to look at Bonnie. "And thank you too, Bonnie. I know this was a bit of a last-minute thing, but you've been a lovely hostess. I– I'm glad to see that Natalie has someone like you."

Bonnie blushed, and Natalie felt a warm glow pulse inside her chest. This was her family. Together. For Christmas.

It wasn't perfect. They were still in their pajamas and dirty dishes still piled high in the sink. The sound from the TV still wafted quietly from the living room and punctuated the awkward silences that stretched between them now and then. But it was still family, and it was still Christmas.

And for now, it was enough.

"I think it's best we get going."

"Yeah." Natalie nodded. "We still need to figure out when we're going to deliver the rest of our Christmas presents, don't we?"

"All those baby clothes for Ethan and Clara," Bonnie agreed.

"She had the baby?" Michelle's eyebrows rose.

"A little girl." Nat smiled. "Sofia Liliana Espinoza."

"You have gifts for her?"

Rafael's eyebrows rose, and he looked over to Michelle, nudging her with his arm.

Michelle gave a slight nod. "We could drop them off for you."

"Really?" Natalie shook her head. "No, we couldn't ask you to do that. We'll figure it out."

"It's no trouble. We'll just leave them on the porch for them. A Christmas surprise." Michelle nodded to Rafael to pick up the bag from under the tree, as if it had been decided. "Just text me the address. You really shouldn't be driving anywhere in your condition. And… it's the least I can do."

Nat and Bonnie looked at each other, and Bonnie shrugged. "It would be nice if we could keep you off the leg for a few days."

"Let me just write up a card for them real quick."

A few minutes and several hugs later, Bonnie and Natalie waved at Michelle's retreating SUV with Ethan and Clara's baby gifts in tow. As they crested past their limited view from inside the foyer, Bonnie at last closed the door and locked it.

"Are we alone now?"

Natalie giggled. "Yes. I'm pretty sure we won't be having any more unexpected visitors."

"Then I finally have you all to myself for Christmas!" Bonnie carefully guided Natalie back to the couch, slipped a hand under her robe, and nuzzled into her neck.

"Honey!" Natalie yelped. Her voice quickly morphed into a moan. "Oh, honey…"

"Yep. Just what I've always wanted."

EPILOGUE

"So let me get this straight. You bribed a tow truck driver out of giving you a ticket by hiring him to pick up and deliver Shawn the Bel Air on the day after Christmas?"

Natalie was in a bit of a grumpy mood from being forced to get up and get dressed at a reasonable hour that morning. The two of them had been up most of the night before exchanging some very *special* Christmas presents.

"Essentially." Bonnie didn't specify the large sum of money she'd paid to make it happen.

Truth be told, she half expected that Ernie wouldn't show up at all, but simply take her money and call it an early Christmas. So she was pleasantly surprised to see a bright red tow truck pull up on Natalie's country road at 9:30 AM, just as they'd negotiated.

When the driver hopped out of the truck, though, it wasn't the middle-aged man that Bonnie had met at the hospital loading entrance. It was a younger man, closer to Natalie's age, wearing a bulky orange hoodie and a ball cap over a mop of curly brown hair and rubbing his hands together.

"I hear you have a car that needs towing?" He called out to her as she met him at the end of the drive.

"You aren't Ernie."

"Nah, Ernie's spending Christmas with his daughter. I'm Beau, I work for him." He stuck out his cold hand. Bonnie shook it.

"Bonnie. Thanks for coming by on such short notice."

"It's no problem! Now where's this car?"

Bonnie led him to the garage, where she and Natalie had just finished unearthing the 1954 Chevy Bel Air from the last remaining piles of junk. Beau let out a low whistle.

"Well, it's not everyday you see something like this," he observed. "She's a beaut!"

"So I hear." Natalie patted the hood affectionately. "We gotta get this baby to Shawn's parent's house in West Virginia. Apparently he's camped there for the holidays."

Natalie watched as Beau backed the tow truck into the driveway and rigged up the winch to pull the car onto the trailer. But before he did, Bonnie remembered the second part of her plan.

"Wait! I just need to grab one thing…"

THEY HAD their hazards blinking like Christmas lights as they followed Ernie's Tow Truck through the mountains to get to the tidy subdivision in West Virginia where Shawn's parents lived. They didn't pull up all the way in front of the house though. They'd told Beau that they'd wanted to surprise their friend with the delivery, so instead, Bonnie parked them across the street a few houses down where they could still make out the front door of the two-story, white Colonial. Natalie typed out a text.

"I hope he's up," Bonnie said.

"Oh he's an early riser." Natalie tapped a Santa and a

Christmas tree emoji, then hit send. And just few seconds later, they heard the barbaric yawp of joy.

Shawn practically leapt out of the house, the storm door slamming behind him as he dashed through the snow to where Beau was parked. His smile stretched ear-to-ear as Beau presented his special Christmas delivery.

"Natalie Roche, you sonuva gun! Merry fuckin' Christmas to me!"

"Shawn Joseph Cobb!"

"Sorry, mom!" He shouted back to the door. The garage door opened a moment later, and after a few minutes of musical cars, Beau was lowering the Bel Air into the driveway and Shawn was positively shaking with excitement.

An older man with a walker and an oxygen tank appeared next to Shawn at the door of the garage, and put a hand on his shoulder. Natalie and Bonnie smiled at each other as they witnessed Shawn show off the car to his grandfather, then wave giddily as Beau pulled out of the driveway.

The tow truck slowed down slightly in front of them on its way back out to the road, and Beau gave the two women a salute.

Bonnie gave him a thumbs up, and Natalie waved back.

Still out of sight to Shawn, they observed as he walked around and around the vehicle, checking it out from every angle and opening first the driver's side door, then the others around the car, until he finally got to the hood.

"Here we go," Bonnie hissed under her breath.

He had to grab a screwdriver from the tool bench, but eventually he jimmied it free, wedged the hood open...

And howled as he jumped back in terror.

"What the–?"

"That's our cue!" Natalie squealed, waving her hands at her girlfriend as she revved the sedan back into gear. "Go, go, go!"

Bonnie shoved the toe of her kitten heel into the gas and

they whizzed by his driveway, just in time to see Shawn scramble back to the car and pull out the offending Elf.

"Merry Christmas, Shawn!" The women cried out the window.

"Goddammit, Natalie!"

They could just barely hear the beginning of his mother shouting, "Shawn! Don't take the Lord's name in vain…" as they sped off towards the highway, laughing all the way.

WANNA SEE how Shawn's faring with the Bel Air? Click Here to read on, in Hot Rod Hookups!

ACKNOWLEDGMENTS

A few very special people helped this manuscript come together. I have to thank my husband, Andy, for supporting me in my journey to finish my Fixer Upper Romance series this year. I couldn't have done it without you, honey.

Lindz, thank you so much for your feedback and last-minute fixes that really helped this book come to life. I'm excited to work together more in the future!

Karli, you are my dearest friend and beta reader. I was thinking about you so much while writing this. Thank you for being such a wonderful friend.

All my BookTok buddies and writer friends: whether it's through messages or live comments, you all keep my honest and encourage me to never stop producing. Thank you so much for believing in me and cheering me on. You are so important to me!

Finally, my family: Sue, Momma, Daddy, Kelley… I'm so excited to spend Christmas with all of you this year. Thank you for always believing in me and loving me for who I am.

THANK YOU FOR READING!

Want to see how Shawn's faring with his Christmas present? Check out *Hot Rod Hookups*, available now in ebook, print, and audiobook!

If you enjoyed Bonnie and Natalie's story, please consider leaving a review on your favorite online retailer or social media outlet. Sapphic romances can be really hard to find, and sharing reviews is the best way scientists have found to get the algorithm to show books to their preferred readers. 10/10 dentists recommend it!

And for bonus stories, giveaways, and updates on future books, join my mailing list at www.cassandramedcalf.com/subscribe. I can't wait to share more stories with you!

ALSO BY CASSANDRA MEDCALF

Fixer Upper Romance Series

Betting on the House, Book #1

Betting on the Bird, Book #1.5

Hot Rod Hookups, Book #2

Here Comes the Bride, Book #2.5

ABOUT THE AUTHOR

Cassandra Medcalf is a writer, narrator, audio engineer, food enthusiast, wine taster, do-it-yourselfer, and an amateur film critic (despite barely having seen any movies). She lives on a future vineyard, in a future dream home in upstate New York with her adorable husband and their even more adorable dog. You can follow her and her family's hare-brained schemes and lofty pursuits on her website, cassandramedcalf.com (or, if you're just here for the smut, on TikTok @CassandraMedcalfVO).

Made in the USA
Monee, IL
22 January 2025